HEALING HIS MATE

ALIENS OF OLUURA

BOOK FIVE

IVY KNOX

AUTHOR'S NOTE

If you don't have any concerns regarding content and how it may affect you, **feel free to skip ahead to avoid spoilers!**

This book contains scenes that either reference or depict abduction, human trafficking, abuse, graphic violence, as well as substance abuse, which may be triggering for some. If you or someone you know is in need of support, there are places you can go for help. I have listed some resources at the end of this book.

CHAPTER 1

NALBA

My bare feet slap against the tiled floors of our hallway as I chase Ekoya down the steps and out the front door.

"Sisters are supposed to share!" she shouts over her shoulder.

"Slow down, girls," I hear my father say in a flat, bored tone as we pass him on the stone pathway. He carries his hunting gear over his hunched shoulders. I have never seen him anything but exhausted. That is when he is home, which is not often.

"You already had yours! That is mine!" I shout back at Ekoya as she shoves another large piece of junasii bread into her mouth. I will never understand how she is able to run at top speed while eating. Her ability to multitask has always been impressive, since the moment she took her first steps while patting her chubby hand against a toy drum. Perhaps I would be more in awe of her if I were not filled with rage that she has stolen my bread. Not that I have any wish to take it back. Certainly not after her grubby hands have been all over it.

Though the scent of warm bread still fills my nose despite the fresh air.

She takes a hard left down a narrow dirt alley, and I struggle to keep up. When did she get faster than me?

I notice the loosened laces of her boots flapping in the wind and whipping against her slim calves. "Slow down!" I command Ekoya, keeping my eyes focused on her feet. She should have tied her laces before we left our home. She always forgets and I have to do it for her. It is quite frustrating.

She ignores me, leaping over a fallen tree branch and charging toward the gray sand beach of the Vtria sea. "Catch me!" she eventually yells back with a mouth full.

I hear splashing up ahead as I duck and weave past the wall of thick brush that separates the heart of Oovahr City from the seaside. The beach is occupied, it seems. And I will revel in the embarrassment my younger sister will feel once I tackle her to the ground for her thieving ways in front of an audience.

The moment Ekoya emerges into the clearing, she trips on the laces of her boot and falls into the sand, face first. Her little arms flail as she pulls herself up, but her hands go to her throat immediately as she coughs and inhales sharply.

"What?" I ask her. "Are you choking?" Of course, she is. She should not run with food in her mouth. I have told her many times. Ekoya's cheeks hollow as her eyes turn wild, and she points to her throat.

My heart stops. I do not know how to help her. I have not been trained in this.

Frantically, I slap the middle of her back as I encourage her to keep coughing.

"What do I do?" I shout as I grip Ekoya's arm. "Help!"

"Move!" says a blur who shoves me aside. I stumble to regain my footing, and when I look up, I see Prince Varrek with his arms wrapped around Ekoya's middle. He clasps his hands together in front of her and yanks them inward causing Ekoya's eyes to bulge.

"What are you doing!" I yell at the prince. I have not spoken to him before, but I have heard all about the king's dashing son, who has just begun warrior training and will one day become the ruler of Trovilia. His title means nothing to me though, especially if he kills my sister right before my eyes. I will end him if he does not save her.

Another boy, whose name I do not know, runs up beside him and corrects Prince Varrek's form. I believe I have seen him at the market buying food with his mother. "You must strike up and in," he says. His mane is long and black, and he flips it casually over his bare, wet shoulder as he watches the prince try again. This time, it dislodges the chunk of bread from Ekoya's throat, which goes flying across the beach. Ekoya wraps both hands around her throat as she takes quick, deep breaths.

"T-thank you," she whispers.

She is breathing. She will live.

As relieved as I am to see that, anger at how close she came to death washes over me like a wave. "How many times have I told you not to run with food in your mouth? And that was my *bread, you little monk slug!"*

Ekoya shows no remorse. She does not regret a thing. "You did not catch me," she replies with a sly grin through ragged breaths.

On the brink of death, she cares for nothing beyond beating me in a foot race. I worry about anyone who crosses her path once she is grown. I cannot even be angry with her for it because I am too astonished by all that I have just witnessed.

I open my mouth to reply, but laughter comes out instead. She joins me, and Prince Varrek looks between us, confused and mildly entertained, it seems.

"You are welcome," he mumbles as he strides away with the other boy.

I narrow my gaze at the future king with his shimmery silver hair and his growing muscles. He is too confident for my liking. "I should thank your friend. He is the real savior here, is he not?"

The prince turns and puts his hands on his hips. "I suppose that is true." His mouth curves up into a subtle smile.

"Thank you for your assistance, young warrior," I say to the black-haired boy, adding a dramatic bow to show my respect.

The boy laughs and places a hand over his heart. "'Twas an honor to be of service." As I turn to continue scolding Ekoya, I am ripped away . . . into darkness.

"Irksome little beast," I murmur to no one.

"Nalba, you're awake!" a creature with smooth brown skin says as she smiles down at me. I cannot place her, but she addresses me as if we are close.

I jerk back instinctively, but as I am in a bed, there is nowhere for me to go but deeper into my pillow. "Wha- w-who are you?" I screech in response. My eyes adjust to the bright light hanging above, and when I scan my surroundings, I become even more confused. This is not a room I have been in before. "Did we crash? Where is Varrek?"

"Uh, crash?" the creature asks. "Varrek is probably with Chloe."

Cloh-ee? Who is Cloh-ee?

"Nalba!" another voice exclaims. Within moments, Kaiva is taking my hand in hers and brushing my mane off my forehead. "You have come back to us! I am relieved," she says with a sigh.

Come back? Where did I go?

"Kaiva," I say, warily eyeing the other creature I do not recognize. "What is happening? And who is that?"

"My dear, that is Aye-vah, the human female who is my son's mate," she replies as if that information means anything to me. "Ahlvo . . . my son."

"Yes, I know your son, Kaiva." Of course, I know who her son is. Frustrated, I go to slam my head down on my pillow, but I feel a throbbing pain on the side of my head I did not notice before.

"Careful," Kaiva says as she lightly touches the side of my scalp. I wince at the contact. "You are still healing from a head injury."

"You gave us quite a scare!" this Aye-vah says. When I do not reply, she adds, "You got thrown into a tree and landed head-first on a rock during the battle with Bzzsil Chi. Remember? You've been asleep for four days."

I close my eyes, trying to comprehend all they have told me. I find no memories of being hurled into a tree. Did this happen on Trovilia? No, that is not possible. I woke up early this morning and boarded the ship to take us to our new planet. Oluura, I think it is called. That, I remember. Nothing of the sort occurred before our ship launched into the sky.

Was this tree on the ship, perhaps?

No. No, I would have remembered such a strange thing. Our ship was big enough to fit the members of our new clan, Varrek, and the rest of his crew once we were able to meet them in space, but not large enough to contain any sort of nature sanctuary.

Frustrated at the hole in my memories, I run my fingers along the creases in my furrowed brow. "Can you please get Varrek? I must speak with him." He will have the answers I need. And clearly, he is here, which means he is alive and well. Even if our ship did crash, he survived. Yes. Yes, Varrek will know what this whole "tree" incident is about, and how I ended up here.

Kaiva and Aye-vah exchange a concerned glance, then Kaiva lightly touches my shoulder and tells me they will return shortly. The two of them do not go far. I can hear them whispering to one another from across the room.

I drift off to sleep before Kaiva and Aye-vah return.

* * *

When I awaken, the brown-skinned creature from before is at my side again. What was her name?

"You're back!" she says excitedly, then points to her chest, "Aye-vah."

Ah, that is right. Mated to Ahlvo.

She hands me a cup of water, and I drink it down in one gulp. "So, Kaiva went to check on Chloe, but she'll be back soon. In the meantime, I was hoping we could try something."

It hurts to narrow my gaze, so I sit silently, waiting for her to continue.

"Does that sound okay?" she asks with wide eyes, nodding up and down in an exaggerated way that looks utterly ridiculous.

"Yes," I reply slowly, mimicking her nod.

She chuckles and says, "Okay. First off, can you tell me your name?"

"Nalba," I say with an impatient huff.

Aye-vah nods, pleased with my answer. "Good. Good. Can you tell me where you are?"

"In a room I do not recognize. Beyond it, I assume we have made it to Oluura, yes?" I ask. I should be assisting the clan with setting up our new home. Or exploring this new planet. There is much to be done.

"Um, yes," Aye-vah begins, pausing to bite her lip, "We're on Oluura." Then she clears her throat and scribbles something on the screen pad in her hands. "And what year is it?"

Briefly, the answer escapes me. The year is not something we paid much attention to on Trovilia. Our focus was more on the current season, and the one to come. But then I remember. "It is the year forty-two thousand six hundred three."

Aye-vah drops the screen pad onto the bed. "Hmm, yeah. This isn't working. I guess I didn't realize how your answers could differ from mine."

The door swings open and Varrek enters. A gust of wind sweeps by him, lifting the ends of his long silver hair off his shoulders. He shuts the door and lets out a deep exhale. "It gets colder by the day, it seems," he says to Aye-vah, then his eyes land on me. "Ah, Nalba! You are back. I am pleased to see this."

"Varrek, thank god you're here," Aye-vah exclaims. "I tried testing Nalba's memory, but I need you to fact-check her answers."

"I do not know what that means, but I am happy to help," he replies, then gives me a nod. He looks . . . different. Mostly the same, but there are creases around his mouth I do not remember seeing. And he looks tired, as if restful slumber has evaded him for many moons.

"You do not look well, Varrek," I tell him.

He barks out a laugh, and says, "Well, thank you, Nalba. It seems you are feeling just fine. Shall I go then?"

Aye-vah chuckles, too, but I do not understand the joke. "The perils of living with a newborn."

Newborn?

"So, Nalba, can you tell me what year it is again?" Aye-vah asks, clasping her hands together.

I sigh and drop my head, carefully this time, back on the pillow. "Forty-two thousand six hundred three," I repeat.

Varrek jerks his head back and gives me a questioning glance. "That is wrong. If we were still going by Trovilian time, the year would be forty-two thousand six hundred *eight*."

"What?" I ask, popping my head up. "That is impossible." I have never been skilled at timekeeping, but there is no way I would miscalculate it that much.

"What's the last thing you remember, Nalba?" Aye-vah asks, her tone turning serious. "Before you woke up here."

My memories of that last day on my home planet flood in, and my heart twists at the view of Trovilia in the distance from the ship we are leaving on. "I woke up early and loaded my belongings onto the ship that Varrek secured for the new clan," I tell them. "We settled into our quarters on the ship, and later that day, we met you and your crew in space. You had set bombs on the *Striker* before you transferred to our ship, and the moment they detonated, everyone on the ship cheered."

I remember the pride that surged through me knowing Varrek executed his plan to sabotage his father's mission flawlessly. As far as the evil King Muryk knew, his only son was dead, along with his entire crew of warriors, and his largest vessel had been destroyed. There would be no feasible way for him to continue pursuing his mission to kidnap females from D'Alluk and force them into a breeding program.

He wanted revenge against the neighboring planet for unknowingly spreading a deadly virus to our citizens—a virus that killed many of our people, mostly females, including Ekoya. But that is not how sickness works.

The D'Allukan tourist who carried the virus did not know he had it. He also did not know it was a disease our people were not immune to. I always understood King Muryk's anger and where it came from. He lost his wife. I lost my sister. If I could murder a virus, I would do so. That is not something I am capable of, though. I learned to live with the pain. And the opportunity to begin anew on Oluura, far from the place I suffered and grieved, was thrilling. I remember going to sleep on that ship with excitement in my heart.

"That's . . . the last thing you remember?" Aye-vah asks me, breaking through my thoughts.

"Yes," I reply.

"Nalba," Varrek begins, scratching his chin, "We settled on Oluura a long time ago."

"Five years, right?" Aye-vah adds.

Varrek nods. "Correct."

My eyes dart back and forth between the two of them, not understanding.

"You have no memory of building a home here? Or your shop? Or the humans arriving?" Varrek asks nervously.

"Or any of your inventions?" Aye-vah adds with a hopeful smile.

Pinching my eyes shut, I try to picture it all—the home, the shop, faces that look similar to Aye-vah's. I find nothing. "N-no," I mumble. "I recall none of that."

Aye-vah blows out an unsteady breath and picks up her screen pad once again. "Nalba, I'm so sorry to be the one to tell you this, but I think you have amnesia."

CHAPTER 2

NALBA

*A*mnesia. How could such an overwhelming experience be simplified into a one-word diagnosis? It does not make sense to me.

"How do I retrieve my memories?" I ask, trying to ignore the bile rising in my throat and the panic that is causing my hands to quiver. "And how long will it take?" If I have been here for five years, I must have projects I am working on. Inventions I must complete. I need to resume my work immediately.

The moment Kaiva returns, Aye-vah tells her about my lost memories, then she starts looking over my brain scans once again. "There is some swelling here," she says, showing me the image of my brain tissue and pointing to the puffier section on the left. "But it has already gone down a bit since the first scan. That is a good sign."

"And what of my memories?" I ask again.

Kaiva's head drops slightly. "I do not know when they will return. I am hopeful it will be soon, Nalba."

Aye-vah clears her throat and gently bumps her elbow into Kaiva's. "There is a chance…a very small chance . . ." Kaiva reluctantly adds, "they will not return at all. But there is no need to think about that now. You are recovering."

Breath has left my body. My limbs feel heavier, as if steel weights are attached to the ends, pulling me deeper into the thin cushion of the bed.

What am I without a properly functioning mind? *Who* am I? My entire life, I have been praised and sought after for my innovative creations. It is why I was chosen as lead apprentice by Yignnuf, the most talented inventor on Trovilia, and worked by his side until his death. It is why Varrek asked me to leave Trovilia and join his new clan on Oluura. If I cannot contribute to the clan in that way, what will become of me?

"Nalba? Are you unwell?" Varrek asks, gently shaking my shoulder.

"Of course, I am unwell!" I shout back. "There must be something you can do. A medicine you can give me. A procedure . . . something," I beg Kaiva in a shaky whisper. "Please." My lip trembles and I bunch the blanket in my fist in an effort to hold back tears. I do not cry. I have not cried since Ekoya's death, and I will not cry this day. Yignnuf would be disgusted by this emotional display I am putting on.

"Nalba. Nalba, shhh," Kaiva says in a soft, comforting voice. "You will heal, my dear. But you must be patient. Give your brain time, and your memories will return to you."

"There are things we can do to help, you know," Aye-vah says, her eyes bright and eager. "Ways to trigger those memories."

My fingers find a loose thread on the blanket, and I focus my nervous energy on tugging at it. I am desperate to get my mind back to where it was. "How?" I ask, my voice cracking at the end. "I will do anything."

"For starters, Varrek," she says as she turns to look at him, "why don't you fill Nalba in on what's happened since her last memory on the ship up to the day the girls and I arrived."

His eyes drop to his feet, lips pursed. "What if I do not remember all that has happened during that time? Nalba and I were not together often. I worry I am not the right person to provide her this information."

Aye-vah smiles and waves a dismissive hand. "I'm not expecting you to remember every detail. Just fill in the blanks a bit. Right now, that time frame for her is an empty void. Give her a general overview."

"What do you mean *we were not together often*?" I ask Varrek. I have clear memories of us as pleasure mates back on Trovilia, and then that time a few eves before we boarded the ship to Oluura that he shared my bed. Has that ended? "Have we discontinued our mating?"

"Well, yes, Nalba," Varrek replies as if the answer should be obvious. When he notices my furrowed brow, he adds, "We have not been pleasure mates since before we left Trovilia. And I am mated to Clohee, a human female. We have a child together."

My mouth falls open. "You are mated? To a . . . human?" I ask, failing to hide my shock. "You are a father?"

He smiles widely, showing almost all of his gleaming white fangs. Fangs that sunk into my shoulder during our last mating mere days ago, but in reality, several years ago. How strange to hold the flutter of arousal for this male when he has long forgotten those very feelings he held for me.

Though, I suppose it is good that he found his inara. I was never meant to be that for him. His cock is delightful. The way it is shaped fit inside me perfectly, and when he would vibrate, his cock would rub against my *k'billita* in all the right ways. The rest of him, however, I can hardly stand most days. Varrek feels too intensely for me. He is a dramatic male. Every experience is either sheer magnificence or extreme disappointment. Nothing occurs between the two. I found it quite irritating.

"It is good," I tell him, "that you have someone who will tolerate you for the rest of time. She must be a patient and understanding creature. I am pleased by this news." I mean every word I speak. I shall miss the use of his cock, but as the leader of the clan, he needs a strong female by his side to guide him, comfort him, and prioritize the clan's needs. He cannot do that alone.

He laughs and nods in appreciation. "That is one of the nicest things you have ever said to me, Nalba. I thank you."

"You're actually pretty tight with Chloe," Aye-vah says. "She works for you."

That surprises me. I have never had many friends, and certainly not of another species. "Truly?"

"Yes," Varrek answers. "You convinced me to rescue her after it was discovered that she was taken by my father the night of our last Maevstra celebration."

"Your father kidnapped her?" I ask, my voice rising in volume with each word. Varrek's father locating us was his biggest fear. He always said if his father found us on Oluura, he would kill us all. "He knows you are alive? How did he find us? Do we need to leave?"

Varrek sighs heavily and runs a rough hand through his silver mane. "He did find us, then he took my inara and locked her in a dungeon beneath the castle. Ahlvo and I traveled to Trovilia to confront him," he puts a hand on top of mine, "and now he is dead. We no longer live in fear of my father's wrath."

"You killed him!" I squeal. He should have done so when his father first went mad and showed signs of ruthless, fascistic views. We would not have had to leave Trovilia at all. But as long as the king is dead, life for Trovilian citizens is no doubt better than it was under his rule.

"Actually, Ahlvo did," he replies with a sly grin, "but not before my father shot him in the leg. The bullet was coated in flesh-eating bacteria. It nearly killed him."

Oh, Ahlvo. He is a good male and the warrior with the strongest thirst for blood. I am not entirely surprised that he was injured in the confrontation. Ahlvo has spent most of his days on the front lines, eager to defend his people and his homeland. It is a wonder he was not severely injured in battle until now. I am glad he survived, however. His heart is kind. "He is recovering, then?"

"He is," Aye-vah replies with a dip of her chin. "It took a while, but he's able to walk again, and we're dealing with the bouts of depression as they come. But we owe you a lot, Nalba. That cane you made him gave him the hope he needed to keep trying."

"The cane . . . I . . . made?" I ask, once again surprised by the information provided. It does not sound like a project I would typically take on. Although, being friendly with Varrek's inara does not sound like me either.

"Yes! He loves it," Aye-vah exclaims. "He trains with it as often as his body will allow."

"Why would he train with a cane?" I ask, confused. I imagine it would be an effective way to bludgeon an opponent, but an odd choice for a preferred weapon.

"Because it turns into a sword! He just presses a button and boom," she says, clapping her hands together, "he goes from limping cane-carrier to bad-ass sword wielder. It transforms him, Nalba. He instantly stands straighter. He looks stronger. You gave him that."

"Oh" is all I can say as I swallow the lump in my throat. Praise is not a new thing for me. I get it constantly for my work. So why are Aye-vah's words affecting me this way? It must be the head injury.

I rub my eyes, trying to absorb this new information. It is a lot to comprehend. "I think I would like to sleep."

"Of course, dear," Kaiva says, then looks at Varrek and Aye-vah and nods toward the door.

"Sorry, Nalba. We didn't mean to overwhelm you," Aye-vah says in a soft tone.

"My apologies," Varrek adds.

I shake my head. "No, it is fine. It is just . . . a strange thing to hear about a life I have already lived, but do not remember."

"I can't even imagine," Aye-vah mutters. Her expression is one of awe and genuine concern. She is good, this human. I like the idea of her with Ahlvo.

Kaiva pats my arm and heads upstairs as the others head toward the door. Before they reach it, the door swings open and a large male enters holding two plates piled high with food and a bowl lodged in the crook of his elbow. "Greetings, Nalba! I am here to deliver your evening meal!" He beams at me.

He is familiar, in a way. I have seen him before. Images flip through my head with him on Trovilia, then boarding the ship with the rest of the clan. I smile as he places one plate on my lap and the other two on the metal tray at my side. He hands me a utensil and shoots me a wink. "One of your favorites," he says in a jovial tone as he gestures toward the pile of shredded brown meat surrounded by yellow blobs of mush.

"Many thanks," I say with a nod. "And who are you?"

CHAPTER 3

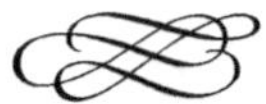

WALDRIC

Nalba does not remember me. The female I crave, the one my heart beats for, does not know who I am. I continue to stare at her, not knowing what to say. This feels like the cruelest of jokes.

"Uh, Waldric?" Aye-vah says, grabbing my attention. "Nalba is suffering from post-traumatic amnesia and doesn't remember the last five years. The last thing she remembers before waking up this afternoon is boarding the ship from Trovilia to Oluura."

My mouth suddenly feels dry. I swallow and attempt to breathe normally, despite the shallow exhales that continue to rush out of my body. "You remember nothing?" I ask Nalba. She shakes her head slowly, and it is then that I realize how small she looks, lying there with a bandage covering half her scalp. How fragile. Her bones may be stronger than a human female's, but she is not immortal.

It is quite possible she is lucky to be alive at all after being thrown against that tree.

But I cannot tell her that. Not now. She looks stricken by her diagnosis. She must have no idea what our village even looks like. The home she has built and a community she has been an integral part of— gone from her mind.

I wish to tell her all that has occurred since that day we boarded Varrek's ship, our eyes meeting as we strapped into our seats to prepare for takeoff. The sparks that burst through my chest and behind my eyes when she smiled at me. And the many smiles she has lit up the Oluuran sky with since that day.

With the way her shoulders are hunched forward, though, it is clear that kind of information would only overwhelm her. If I am to ease the clench from her fists, I must comfort her.

"I am called Waldric," I tell her, placing a hand over my heart. "I am the clan's cook. And this," I point to the plate of roasted *kuhnypa* with a savory b'fiko berry glaze in her lap, "is one of your favorite dishes. Well, it was. It would do me a great honor if you would taste it and confirm that has not changed."

Her soft lips curl up on one side, forming a slight smile. I feel as victorious to win that smile as I did during my days as a warrior defeating the enemy. Nalba scoops a pile of it onto her spoon and moans with bliss the moment she closes her mouth around it.

"Mmm, so succulent, Waldric," she says, still chewing. Once she swallows, she says, "Do you make this each day? Because I am certain I would never tire of it."

I chuckle, dipping forward in a bow. "Many thanks for your compliments. I am pleased your tastes have not changed." I regret my words the moment they are out because they are sure to remind her of her condition, which I was deliberately trying to avoid.

If Nalba is hurt by the reminder, she does not show it. She tilts her head to the side with a snicker. "It is the only thing that has not changed, it seems."

"Well, we'll let you enjoy your meal and rest up," Aye-vah says as she and Varrek edge closer to the door.

I would stay by her side if I could. Nothing would bring me more joy than to watch her eat the food I prepared, but it does not feel appropriate. Moments ago, I was a stranger to her. Her memories from the last five years are locked away in some deep, dark corner of her extraordinary mind, and she cannot access them. It must be unthinkably terrifying for her.

"I will leave you now," I say, covering my heart with my hand once again. "Sleep deep, Nalba."

"Wait," she calls out mid-bite. "Sleep . . . deep?"

I turn and shrug in response. "It is what my mother used to tell me when I was a child."

"I like it," she says, a thoughtful expression flashing across her face. "Very much."

"As do I."

I close the door to Kaiva's med room behind me as I brave the cold evening air to walk back to the food hall. Krahn, one of our hunters, has been serving the final meal to the clan in my absence so I could bring Nalba hers. I pat him on the back when I return, and he gives me a nod before striding over to assist Elle-noor at the dish station. He is not the best cook. He is not a good cook at all, actually, but he enjoys it more than hunting, so I allow him to assist me.

There is also an understanding between us. A shared desire. I was a warrior on Trovilia, but it was not how I wanted to spend my days. I trained and continued with it because my father was also a warrior, and it is the path he wished for me to follow. But coming to Oluura gave me the chance to be someone else. Someone new. Cooking soothes my soul. It nourishes my people. It keeps them alive. Being the clan's cook is an honor, and I get the sense that Krahn would make that same choice and leave his hunting days behind him, given the opportunity.

It may not be a coveted role to many, but it is to us.

"How'd it go?" Elle-noor asks as she approaches, wiping her wet hands on a clean rag. "Did she swoon?"

"No," I reply with a sigh. "She does not remember me. She does not remember anything from the last five years."

"What?" Elle-noor asks, jerking her head back. Then her eyes widen as realization hits. "Oh god. Her head injury." Her jaws hang open as her eyes scan the food hall, never settling on anyone or anything. "Five years? She's lost five years of memories?"

"Yes," I tell her. I drop the wooden spoon I was using to stir the pot of stew, frustrated at how powerless I feel. "I do not know what to do. I cannot help her. She looked at my face and there was nothing. Nothing in her eyes to indicate she ever knew me at all."

"I thought she didn't really," Elle-noor says hesitantly. "I mean, no offense, but from the infrequent interactions I've seen, she's never been particularly friendly to you."

I want to correct Elle-noor, but I struggle to find the words to do so, which makes me even more frustrated. "I suppose that is true." Why do I continue thinking of Nalba each day? Why does it seem impossible to forget her? I have asked myself these questions many times.

I turn toward her and huff a breath. "What do you suggest? That I give up?"

She chews on the inside of her cheek, her gaze lifting toward the sky. "I'm curious. Is she your inara? Admittedly, I don't really understand how that bond works among your people."

"You mean the tether," I add.

She nods.

"No, I have not felt the tether. Among our kind, it is something that occurs in both people at the same time, so she would feel it as well if it existed." I reach up and tuck a loose strand from my mane into the knot atop my head. "She may not be my inara, but I have never cared about such things. I assumed I did not have one at all. And my feelings are not tempered by the lack of tether."

Elle-noor puts her hands on her hips and shifts her weight from her front foot to her back foot, a mischievous smile forming. "Then I think this is an opportunity, Waldric. The best chance you're ever gonna get to win her over."

Her words do not make sense. "What?"

"Think about it," she replies excitedly. "She doesn't know you. She has no idea you've been crushing hard on her for the last five years. All those times you tried to flirt with her and failed. That time you told her you wanted to massage her brain tissue like fresh dough. You remember that, right?"

"Ah, I do, yes."

"She has no memory of that! You can start over. It's like you've been given a second chance!"

A second chance. I like the sound of that. "I can grow close to her by helping her."

"Yes!" Elle-noor squeals as she does a little hop. "You can flirt with her, but like, in a way that won't make anyone cringe. Then she'll see how lovable you are!"

"I do not know how to flirt," I admit. I have tried, many times I have tried, but I get lost in her sparkling gray eyes and forget who I am or what I wanted to say. "What if her memories return and she decides I am not worthy of her attention?"

"Then it's time to move on, bud," she replies simply as she returns to her dish station. "You're too much of a catch to chase a woman who doesn't really see you."

It is a nice thought, and not incorrect, but I am not ready to face that reality.

As if reading my thoughts, Elle-noor continues, "But I don't think that'll happen, honestly. Even if her memories come back, you'll be closer to her than you ever were before. That vague idea of who she thinks you are won't hold a candle to the version she's gotten to know." She pulls a wet bowl from the drying tub and begins wiping it with her rag. "This will work."

Two elders approach and I fill their bowls with stew and drop a thick slice of junasii bread on top of each. I think over this plan Elle-noor has, and it does sound intriguing. "When do we begin?"

She makes a clicking sound with her tongue as she places the dry bowl on the table with the rest of the clean, dry dishes. "Right now, my friend. Right fucking now."

CHAPTER 4

NALBA

Kaiva descends the stairs into the med room early the next morning to find me wide awake and restless. "What is wrong, Nalba? Are you in pain?"

"No," I bark out, tired of lying here, staring out the giant windows onto the main path of the village—a place I have no memory of. I wish to explore this new home we have built. I am eager to see my shop and return to my projects. "I am wasting away in this bed. A useless heap of bones and skin. I have things to do, Kaiva."

She chuckles, unbothered by my tone. "Your mind has always been busy, busy, busy. It is a wonder you were able to keep up with it." She gently removes the bandage on the side of my head, checking the wound. She looks pleased. "You are healing well, my dear."

"And . . ." I add, willing her to give me the freedom to leave.

"And I think you should be fine to return to your shop. But–" she presses me down onto the bed the moment I begin to rise, "you must take it slow. Allow yourself the time to get reacquainted with your surroundings. Be kind and patient with yourself. Your body does not work as quickly as your mind."

I nod, agreeing to her terms. "My memories will return once I am in my shop again, yes?"

She pauses, dropping her hands to her sides. She does not answer.

"I spend all my time there, do I not? It is only logical to assume my shop holds the most memories I have made over the last five years. Right?"

She smiles, but it is tight, forced. "Yes, that is a logical assumption, Nalba. And that could indeed happen."

Kaiva's carefully chosen words make me feel better despite the obvious reluctance to agree with me or give me any degree of hope. I know she does not want me to be disappointed if my memories do not return upon entering my shop, but I believe they will. My projects, both completed and in progress, will trigger them.

"Morning!" Aye-vah greets us with a bright smile upon entering the room. She is quite beautiful, Ahlvo's mate. The human face still seems a bit odd to me, structurally speaking, but Aye-vah has a kind of magnetic appeal to her. Your eyes land on her and you want them to stay there.

"Hello," I reply. "I am leaving today! Kaiva has just given me approval to return to my work!"

"Wow, that's wonderful news!" Aye-vah replies as she sets her small shoulder sack on the table closest to the door. "Would you like me to walk you over?"

I am inclined to say no, so I have the chance to explore this unfamiliar place on my own. Any form of exploration is most enjoyable without company, I have found, but I suppose it will help to have someone at my side who can provide names of people and places I have forgotten. "Very well."

"Don't sound so excited," Aye-vah says with a chuckle.

"Did I sound excited? Because I truly am not, but I appreciate your assistance," I tell her honestly.

"Mmm. I do value your candor, Nalba."

I nod. "I am told it is one of my best qualities." Kaiva hands me the boots and pants I came in with, and relief washes over me as I put them on. Though I have only been conscious in the med room for one day, I know I have spent many days here following my injury, and I am eager to return to the life I have been living.

Before Aye-vah reaches for the door, I place my hand on her arm. I turn sideways so I may address both her and Kaiva. "I am happy here, yes? In this place, doing the work I do—would you say I have been happy?"

"Um," Aye-vah replies, hesitantly. "Yeah, I guess so."

"Happy is not the word I would use to describe you, Nalba," Kaiva says. "You are more focused, driven. But I would not say you are unhappy."

I suppose that is an answer. Not necessarily the one I was seeking, but certainly provides a bit of insight. "Ah. Well, thank you."

Following Aye-vah outside, I am immediately taken aback by the lack of direct sunlight. "How does anything grow here?"

Aye-vah tilts her head back, following my gaze. "Yeah, the trees cover most of the village. There are little pockets of sunlight that peek through, though. And we have no trouble with crops. We're also entering the cold season, so sunlight will be less frequent."

My gaze drifts down from the trees to the rooftops and unique designs of each structure surrounding the path we stand on. Each has a completely different shape, different sized windows, doors, and all are built around and against the neighboring trees, giving them the ability to continue growing.

"This is the main path of the village, and from here, you can see pretty much everything," Aye-vah says, gesturing widely with her arms. "That's Varrek and Chloe's house over there." She points to a tall, four-level home situated close to Kaiva's med room. "Me and Ahlvo live in the one sort of diagonally behind it. That narrow path takes you through the forest to the clearing where all the ships are located."

A tall, lanky male with maroon hair and a grimace on his face spots us from a distance, and a bad feeling twists my insides. He is familiar, this male, and clearly a Hexrin, but it is more than just what I remember from the day we left Trovilia. The caution I feel is tied to a more recent moment, a memory I cannot access. "Who is that?" I ask Aye-vah, gesturing toward him.

"Oh," she replies, letting out a sigh of exasperation. "That would be Tibik. He's the self-appointed leader of the Hexrins. We're trying to figure out what to do with him after all the drama during the battle."

I am inclined to ask more questions about him, but I am so distracted by the hate pumping through my blood and the growl rising in my chest that I cannot get the words out. Tibik hears my growl, and the moment his eyes land on me, I flash my lengthening fangs at him, and he quickly scurries back into the forest, the way he came.

"Wait. Do you remember him?" Aye-vah asks, a hopeful note in her voice.

"I do not," I admit. "But I know I do not trust him."

Aye-vah nods. "Not many of us do at this point." She continues naming the residents of each home around the wide path—the names of whom sound vaguely familiar—as two humans (I think that is what they are, anyway), stride past and wave at Aye-vah.

"Hey, girls!" she shouts back, then leans toward me. "Those are two of our newest clan members, Heather and Iris. Six human women arrived a few days ago while you were still unconscious. They were discovered at a brothel on a neighboring planet. It seems like they're settling in pretty well. Ekoya was kind enough to rescue them and send them here since she knew the presence of other humans would comfort them."

Because of the name she just uttered, I am no longer interested in what these humans have endured or how they got here. "You said . . . Ekoya?"

"Yes, Queen Ekoya," she says, nodding emphatically. "You must be so proud of her. Though being related to royalty must be kind of surreal."

"Wh-what . . . I am sorry. I just . . . What did you say?" I stammer. I am not comprehending her words. "My sister is dead. She was the only sibling I had. She died from the virus. I do not—"

"Oh! Oh, fuckity, fuck, fuck. I am so sorry, Nalba. I keep forgetting all the things missing from your memories," Aye-vah replies in a rush, smacking her palm against her forehead. "Okay, so um, Ekoya is alive, and she is now Queen of Trovilia. Varrek's father was keeping her locked in a dungeon beneath the castle. He was planning on using her in his breeding program or whatever. I can't remember the details, but she survived the virus."

The world spins around me and my knees buckle. Suddenly, my fingers are clawing through layers of dirt and squishy blue moss. The air is heavy, and it feels as if I am being pushed down.

She is alive. Ekoya is alive. I never got to say good-bye to her, and she is . . . alive.

"Kaiva!" I hear Aye-vah yell. Her voice is distant now, despite the closeness of her body to mine. "Varrek! Chloe! I need you!"

Moments later, I am covered in hands as I am lifted to my feet. Kaiva's hands are in my hair as she checks my head wound. The rest are placed on my arms and back, offering support. I take it, leaning heavily on them as they guide me toward the structure Aye-vah referred to as mine.

I am placed on a tall stool next to a long steel table that is covered in food scraps, dust, and various tools. This is mine? This mess belongs to me? Yignnuf would have my head if he knew I was leaving my workspace in such disarray.

I do not have the energy to accept that, however, because my entire existence has just been flipped on its head. "You said she is alive? Truly?"

"Yes, Nalba. Ekoya is alive," Varrek replies. "And she is queen."

"But . . . h-how did she survive the virus?" I ask. I cannot make sense of this. "I was told by the healers that she perished. They . . . lied?"

Varrek goes on to tell me how Ekoya developed a condition in the late stages of the virus that made her appear dead, and when she was discovered to be alive, the king saw it as an opportunity to revisit his idea of forcing females to breed in an effort to slowly rebuild the Trovilian race. The virus had decimated it, and this way, he could use females with "pure Trovilian blood" to reproduce under his supervision.

"You say Cruvo saved her?" I ask, astonished. Her mate is a Hexrin, and I have never been fond of him. Or any of the Hexrins. I do not trust their ability to create something out of nothing without the use of data and observations and constant improvements. Real innovation takes time. They do not innovate. They entertain. Nothing more.

"He broke her out of the dungeon, yes. We took down the guards together. Then Ahlvo killed the king," Varrek says, shooting Aye-vah a thankful grin.

"Then Varrek recommended she take the throne, and a majority vote from the council sealed the deal!" a female with a long brown mane, pale skin, and large brown eyes adds excitedly. She has a soft middle, and curves that cover the rest of her body. Her lips are a deep crimson color, and Varrek continues stealing glances at her.

"You are his mate," I say, still in a slight daze. This is too much information to receive in the span of one day. It is only morning and already I am exhausted and confused. "I do not remember your name."

She smiles, exposing her little blunt teeth. "Hi, Nalba, I'm Chloe. I work with you here as your assistant, but I'm also your bestie."

"Behs-tee?" I repeat slowly. That word is not translating for me.

"Best friend," Cloh-ee clarifies, her cheeks turning bright pink. She seems slightly nervous, which I suppose is fair since she just had to introduce herself to someone who she considers a friend.

"I see," I say, looking down at my still-shaking hands. Then I remember why they started shaking in the first place. "Ekoya. Can you contact her? I must see her face."

"Certainly," Cloh-ee says at the same time Varrek says, "No."

"I believe she is still visiting D'Alluk to work on the peace treaty," Varrek adds.

Cloh-ee scoffs, and her eyes roll to the side. "Ekoya has one sister, and that's Nalba—who has amnesia. She also just learned that Ekoya's not actually dead. I think the queen can spare a moment for the sake of her sister's mental health."

Varrek considers this silently for a moment, then his chin dips as he looks down at her in awe. "You are right, inara."

Impressive.

She reaches up on her toes to kiss Varrek's cheek, then takes his screen pad from his vest pocket. Within moments, the face of my only sister fills the screen.

"Nalba, dear! You are awake!" she shouts in greeting. "I have not slept well since your accident. How is your head wound? Is it healing properly?"

A gasp escapes me, and tears blur my view of her perfect, round face. "I-it is true," I mumble as I wipe my tears away. They continue to fall, though, because before me sits a miracle. "I did not believe it, but you are here. Alive."

"Ekoya, Nalba has amnesia," Cloh-ee says as she leans over my shoulder. "She doesn't remember the last five years. So you being alive is clearly a shock to her."

When the Trovilian healers came to collect Ekoya and take her to the medical center for treatment of the virus, her skin was a pallid, drab yellow. Her golden sheen had disappeared, she was thin and frail, and could barely hold her eyelids open. They told us she was dead five days later. Now, here she sits with shiny black hair plaited to one side, eyes bright and sparkling, and a crown atop her head.

"I am so p-proud to be your sister. Please know that," I sniffle. I am now sobbing, and though I can hear Yignnuf's stern voice in my head telling me to shield my weakness, I cannot help it.

She smiles, catching a single tear as it slides down her cheek. "You said this the last time."

"Said what?" I ask.

"After I escaped the dungeon and was crowned queen, the first time we spoke, you said the very same thing."

"Well," I say, wiping my dripping nose, "it is the truth."

"I am proud of you as well," she says. "This cannot be easy, losing your memories, but I know they will come back to you."

"What if . . ." I begin, then suck in a breath almost too afraid to say it out loud, "what if they do not?"

"Then you will adapt," she replies simply. "I must go. I am dining with the rulers of D'Alluk in their garden this morning. Much to do to secure the treaty. You have my heart, Nalba," she says as she gives me a final warm smile before disconnecting the comm.

I continue to stare at the black screen, wondering if I imagined it. Varrek hands me a cloth from his pocket, and I use it to wipe the lingering drips from my nose and eyes. Cloh-ee eventually returns the screen pad to Varrek, and he and Kaiva bid farewell before returning to their duties. Aye-vah and Cloh-ee, however, remain at my side.

My eyes land on Cloh-ee, then drift to Aye-vah, as I wait for them to speak.

"Would you like a proper tour of your home?" Cloh-ee asks, sweeping her arms in front of her.

Right. This was supposed to be an important moment—the first time I take in the place I have called home over the last five years. Any scrap of hope I have about my memories returning rests on whether being in this space triggers them. I was too distracted when they dragged me in here to have a proper look around.

"Yes," I say, rising to stand, "indeed." My knees remain a bit shaky, but that is probably from the shock of learning my sister is alive. I place my hands over my eyes as I step toward the front door, then I turn to face the entirety of my shop. Taking a deep inhale, I hold it for a moment before releasing the breath. I drop my hands and slowly open my eyes.

I see several long metal tables with matching metal boxes stacked beneath. There are three stools, five orb lights that hang from the high ceilings above, and clutter absolutely everywhere. As my gaze wanders over the messy tabletops, I feel disgust and judgment for the person occupying this space.

How could it be me? How could I possibly find inspiration and work efficiently in this chaos? My workstation at Yignnuf's innovation facility was spotless because anything less would earn you a lashing across the back. Knowing cleanliness was a requirement, I remember growing fond of the monotonous task of tidying my space before and after each shift.

What caused me to evolve into a person who does not respect my surroundings?

"Anything coming back to you?" Aye-vah asks quietly.

I scan the room again, clenching my jaw as I silently beg for a flicker of recognition. Something. Anything.

Eventually, I reply, "Nothing."

Cloh-ee places a hand between my shoulder blades and rubs back and forth. "Give it time, Nalba. It'll happen."

These females have more hope than I can muster. They are kind for staying with me and reminding me to practice patience. I wish I could.

They guide me up to the second and third levels of my home, which are separate structures entirely. They are connected by a set of wooden steps carved into the thick tree that rests against the backside of my home. The second level is smaller than the first with a square structure made of wood that includes my bedroom and a small washroom. The bed is large and unmade. Given the state of the shop, I should not be surprised by this. There are clothes all over the floor and towels tossed about inside the washroom.

The third level is the smallest, about ten steps above the second level, and contains only one room that is filled with written materials: instructional manuals, historical texts, and copious notes I took from working alongside Yignnuf. Books fill the shelves along each wall, the only break in shelves is the single window that looks out over the second level and the main path of the village.

I ask Aye-vah and Cloh-ee to leave me after a few moments of being inside the book room. If there is a key to the time I have spent on Oluura, I assume it is here, and I wish to discover it alone. These are texts that comforted me on Trovilia, which is why I brought them here. Touching them, scanning through the pages, holding them in my hands—I expect to uncover memories of reading them here in my new home. But the only memories that come are ones from Trovilia.

After flipping through roughly thirteen titles, I find no tangible clues of the person I have been. There is no record of the creations I have been working on, or what I have been doing.

With each I check, my movements become more desperate, my heart picking up speed. "No," I mumble to myself as I toss another aside. I start looking between pages, behind stacks, and on the highest shelves in the room for even a single page of my scribbles from the last five years.

Nothing.

I race down to the second level and rip my bed apart, checking for hidden books beneath pillows, between thick furs, or beneath dirty tunics all over the floor.

Again, nothing.

My ears burn hot with frustration. Beads of sweat form at my temples as I run back to the third floor and check every manuscript again to ensure I missed nothing on the first pass.

"Uhrrahh!" I scream at the ceiling, torn pages crumpled inside my clenched fists.

If I cannot determine how I have spent my time here, how will I continue my work? And if I cannot work, what will I become? *Who* will I become?

CHAPTER 5

WALDRIC

"We have been at this for six days now, and nothing has worked," I say, trying to conceal my agitation from the clan in the food hall as they step in front of me with empty plates in hand, waiting to be served second meal. I scoop a large spoonful of *rinahtunhi* mash onto each plate with a smile as they move through the line. Most days, I enjoy serving my clan in this way. But that is not how I feel today.

"I mean, she is going through a bit of a crisis at the moment. Did you try complimenting her eyes?" Elle-noor asks from the dish station next to me.

"Yes," I reply through gritted teeth. The line in front of me has cleared, so I have a moment to share my honest and obvious vexation. "I hand-deliver each meal to Nalba at her shop. She barely acknowledges my presence, and the times that she has, I get but a moment alone with her before someone interrupts. The most I have gotten is a smile."

Elle-noor sighs. Her small hands are submerged in the soapy dishwater as she scrubs the dishes the clan drops in her bin as they finish eating. "And you've tried shirtless delivery?"

My brow furrows. "Shirtless delivery? You mean, presenting her food with my chest exposed?"

"Yeah."

"No, I have not," I reply as a gust of wind rips through the air and ruffles the loose strands of my mane.

"Ugh, why not?" Elle-noor demands as she stomps her foot.

I shoot her a sideways glance. "Because it is not proper. I do not want her to assume I have just prepared her meal in a state of nakedness."

Elle-noor barks out a laugh. "That's considerate of you, Waldric, but I don't think she'd care. Like, at all. If a hot guy hands me a plate of food, hygiene is not going to be my first thought."

"What would your first thought be then?"

"Hmm," she murmurs as she tilts her head to the side. "Depends on how hungry I am, I guess. But I'd probably be thinking, 'How can I inhale that tasty dish while simultaneously climbing Bruvix like a tree?'"

That causes me to snicker.

"If Nalba showed up at your place topless with a plate of food, what would *your* first thought be?" she asks.

I feel the blood rush to my cheeks, then quickly back down to my cock as my pants tighten around it. I turn slightly to tug at the waistband of my pants, adjusting myself, away from Elle-noor's gaze. When I turn back around, Elle-noor shoots me a knowing smirk. Clearing my throat, I reply, "I would not notice the food at all."

"Exactly," she adds. "I say you give it a go. We've tried everything else at this point."

Images of the past several days flip through my mind, following Elle-noor's suggestions to attempt a different approach each time I delivered Nalba's meals: me with my mane down and freshly combed, me wearing a pair of Varrek's significantly tighter pants, telling Nalba how lovely her mane looks, telling her I had a strange dream about her running naked past my home and describing it in vivid detail, offering bottles of ale that I hand-selected to complement the meal, and the most humiliating of all, bumping into her with a mug of water in hand and pretending to accidentally pour it all over my tunic.

Elle-noor was certain that would work. It did not. I wince at the memory of how Nalba looked at me—soaking wet inside her shop, pressing the fabric into my stomach muscles—like I was a complete fool.

Elle-noor crosses her arms over her chest in a huff. "You can't just be like, 'Nalba, I wanna kiss the crap out of your face. Let's give this a shot'?"

"No," I reply. "I cannot."

"Why?"

"I just . . . cannot," I reply. I do not tell Elle-noor about the day, many years ago on Trovilia, when I baked my first *veergahsa* on my own. My mother had been teaching me every dish she knew how to prepare when I returned home between warrior training sessions. We took the veergahsa to the market to see if the local baker would be interested in selling it at his stall.

He agreed and said he would split the credits with me. I was elated. The battlefield did not settle my soul, but the kitchen did. Being able to prepare meals and bake sweet treats between missions with Varrek's crew kept me going until the next time I returned to the kitchen. Longer missions with the crew kept me from my passion, and eventually, I was far too engrossed in the friction between King Muryk and Varrek to cook anything at all.

As we were leaving the market that day, long ago, I spotted Nalba. She was following Yignnuf, her mentor, along with his other apprentices. He was a cold man. Arrogant. Miserable and intent on making those around him miserable as well. I never liked him.

Brilliance means nothing if your soul is a twisted heap of rot.

Yignnuf was buying food at another stall when he stopped to describe the techniques Trovilia's farmers use to grow their crops, and how our local cooks turned the crops into delicious meals for us to eat. One of his apprentices, I am not sure which, asked if cooking was considered a respectable trade. Yignnuf laughed, and loudly proclaimed, "If you lack intelligence, it is."

His apprentices laughed and wholeheartedly agreed. All of them. Nalba too.

That exchange has not dampened my desire for her, but I have not forgotten it.

"I am starting to wonder if it is time to put an end to these foolish games," I say as my gaze lands on the table of six human females Queen Ekoya sent to us. They laugh together as they eat their meals. One of them even waves hello to me when she catches me staring. Ann-ah, I think her name is.

A part of me was terrified to lay my eyes upon them in the chance that one of them was my inara. I did not want confirmation that what I feel for Nalba is a wasted fantasy. Another part of me, however, hoped to feel the tether for one of the humans. Then, my problems would be solved. My focus would shift entirely to wooing one of them, and over time, perhaps they would return my love. I wipe my hands on the rag I keep wrapped around my belt during mealtimes, and say, "I have tried everything to hold her attention. It is done."

Perhaps it is time to give up.

"I am here to assist with middle meal," Krahn says as he enters the food hall. He has assisted me with each meal shift since I began my pursuit of Nalba and has enjoyed it immensely.

"I thank you, Krahn, but you are not needed for this meal," I tell him as the Hexrins and the elders get in line for food.

His face falls at my words, and I feel horrid. He is set to leave shortly for a hunting trip, but if I still require his help, he would be allowed to stay. I know that is what he desires.

"Why don't you try one more time?" Elle-noor suggests as she dries her hands and appears ready to leave her station. "Really pay attention to how she responds. See if she gives you any signals at all that she's interested. If not, then you can move on."

"I do not understand what Elle-noor speaks of, but I agree," Krahn adds, so he can stay and avoid his hunting trip.

I chuckle and pat him on the back as I reach for a plate to fill for Nalba. "Very well. I will try once more," I tell them.

Elle-noor slaps her palm against mine and wishes me luck as she heads toward the falls.

Krahn and I work in companionable silence as we feed the rest of the clan, tuck the remaining servings into the cold box beneath the back counter, and prepare the space for final meal. Taking a moment to wipe the cooking powder and viiki spread off my hands, and also my neck—how did that get there?—I make my way to Nalba's shop with a plate piled high with her favorite snack.

I find two large tr'gory pups sitting outside the front door—one of them Stahn-lee and the other's name I cannot recall—which means Elle-noor is here, and maybe Bruvix as well. There is shouting inside, but it does not deter me.

"Greetings! I have food!" I say, entering with a smile. Striding through the room full of people, I keep my eyes trained on Nalba. "Your favorite, Nalba. Junasii bread with herbs baked in and sweet viiki spread for dipping."

Her cheeks are streaked with tears, but at the sight of food, her expression brightens. She steps toward me and takes a bite, then moans with her eyes pinched shut. The sound jolts my cock to attention, setting my skin ablaze with need.

The moment she swallows, her eyes fly open. "Wait!" she yells, dropping the rest of the bread back onto the plate I am still holding in my hands. She rushes to the metal table behind Cloh-ee and begins digging through a basket beneath it. "I remember. I remember!" she shouts. She pulls out an item that has a curled hook at the bottom of a long wooden handle and grabs Cloh-ee's arm. "Everyone out! Cloh-ee, I need you to note this finding."

She remembered something. Because of . . . me. Because of the food I made. My chest puffs with pride at what I have given her.

Elle-noor, Bruvix, Aye-vah, and Kaiva attempt to leave in a hurry when Cloh-ee says, "Hold up! I'm afraid I can't stay. I have to check on Vahla." She looks pleadingly at Bruvix and Elle-noor. "But perhaps one of you cou–"

"I shall stay," I offer before Cloh-ee can finish speaking. Putting down the plate of bread, I pull out my screen pad. "It would be an honor . . . to provide assistance, Nalba," I add, a new plan taking shape in my head.

"Um, o-kay," she replies, staring at the item in her hand, not noticing my lingering presence. But then she lifts her chin, and her eyes meet mine. They hold a fierce determination. "Yes," she says, her lips slowly parting. She runs her tongue along the bottom lip, then the top.

She smiles. "Yes, this is the key. I need you. And your food. I need you here with me."

CHAPTER 6

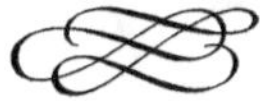

NALBA

It was fleeting, and nothing more than a single image, but it was there. I hold onto the memory as if I can trap it in my hands while I run to the table in the center of my shop and pull out a box from the shelf beneath it. Sucking in a breath, I carefully lift the item from the box. It is a *pullobyskahn,* a new weapon I am working on that shoots curved metal hooks from a hollow wooden block with propulsion similar to that of bullets from a gun.

But . . . that cannot be the entire point of this weapon, can it? The design lacks innovation. It needs something more. A unique element that makes it a truly dangerous weapon. The end result is a hook-shaped bullet. That is all.

Is this what I do now? Create useless trinkets that are not even pleasant to look at?

"What is it?" the cook asks as he stands at my side. I forgot he was here. But I was the one who demanded that he stay, after all.

I let out a sigh, tossing the pullobyskahn and the loading block back into the box and return the box beneath the table. "It is an incomplete project. A disappointing one." I throw myself onto the nearby stool and place my head in my hands. "I remembered it," I murmur, shaking my head. "I remembered the name, and I could see myself loading the hooks into the block. But that . . . cannot be a completed design. It cannot."

The cook, Waldric, I believe his name is, places the plate of bread next to me and leans his hip against the table. "Do not let this moment feel like defeat, Nalba," he says in a comforting tone. "You remembered something. That is extraordinary. This is just the beginning."

I lift my head at his words. "It is?"

"Yes," he says, gifting me with a hopeful grin. In fact, this male seems to emanate hope from his entire body. "You should be very proud of your progress."

"Th-thank you," I stammer, not knowing how to respond.

When I would have a setback such as this in Yignnuf's innovation facility, he would not offer kind words. That was not his approach at all. He would push me deeper into my melancholy with harsh comments about my waning creativity or how mediocre my finished projects have been until I was so angry that it fueled my need to continue working in order to make improvements. That was how he treated all of his apprentices, but he was particularly tough on me.

"Would you like more?" Waldric asks as he lifts the plate of bread in front of me.

I nod, taking the corner off the top piece in the stack and popping it into my mouth. Perhaps more memories will return if I continue eating.

"If you remember nothing else, do not fret," he says as if he can read my thoughts. He uses his thick forearm to sweep the crumbs off the table and into his large hand. "They will come. You know that for certain now. Just wait for them."

"But I do not have time to wait. The clan . . . the clan does not have time to wait," I explain. "They are counting on me."

He places both palms on the end of the table and leans forward, holding my gaze. "The clan is counting on you to prioritize your recovery. We want you to care for yourself."

He is quite a large male, this Waldric. He may even be the largest male in the clan. He may not be the tallest—that is Varrek, I believe— or the strongest—which is Ahlvo—but he is certainly the widest and thickest of them all. Waldric has the sheer mass of a formidable warrior, despite being a cook. Everything else about him is far too kind to incite fear, however, like his eyes. They are a mix of burnt orange and auburn with flecks of blue scattered close to the pupil. How did I not notice his eyes before?

"Are you well, Nalba?" he asks, breaking through my trance.

I gently run my fingers over the long wound on my scalp that runs from behind my ear to the back of my head. "Uh, yes. I am fine."

Waldric brushes his palms together, wiping the breadcrumbs from his hands, then crosses his arms across his wide chest. "How else can I be of service to you?"

"Service?" I repeat slowly as my eyes follow the path of a vein running from his right wrist to the underside of his forearm, disappearing behind the rolled sleeve of his tunic.

"You said you wanted me to stay."

That shakes me to a state of awareness. "Yes, right," I say, clearing my throat, forcing my mind to focus on the task at hand. "I am hopeful that continuing to eat the foods I have enjoyed here on Oluura will help me recover my memories. I would like for you to prepare meals for me here and remain until after I have finished eating. This way, we can determine precisely which foods are the strongest triggers, and I can focus on eating those exclusively to get my mind back to where it was."

His brow furrows as he scans each wall and corner of my shop.

"There are other cooks that can take your place at the food hall, yes?" I ask, caught off guard by the slight tremble in my voice. Why am I nervous?

"Yes, there is another cook here."

That is technically an answer to my question, but I suppose I should make my needs clearer. "So, you will stay? You will cook for me? Each meal?"

My heart drops into my stomach when he purses his lips. He is going to say no. But I need him. I need my mind back, and his food is the only thing that has led me to my memories.

"It is just that . . ." he begins.

But I do not let him finish. "Please," I say, getting to my feet and standing before him. I take one of his hands. It envelops mine until I cannot see my fingers at all. "I am begging you. Please, help me."

Waldric swallows as his gaze lifts from our joined hands to my eyes. "Yes," he whispers. "Yes, I will help you. It would be an honor."

I press my lips to his knuckles and let out a relieved sigh. "Thank you." Then I release him and return to my bread. I tear it down the center and shove the smaller piece into my mouth. Once I am done, I clap my hands together. "You may set up your cook station here," I say, gesturing to the metal table along the far wall. At the end of the table is a fire pit he can use to cook the food. "Feel free to bring your supplies and begin setting up."

"Uh, very well," he says, his voice a husky rumble as he nods and takes four long strides to exit my shop. I cannot help but notice his ample, but firm, backside as he leaves. It has the shape of two humongous b'fiko berries pressed together and concealed by the fabric of his pants. My core heats as I picture digging my heels into it as he slams his cock into me.

How odd. My body has not reacted this way for a male besides Varrek in ages.

I shake my head as I grab my screen pad from the table and send a comm to Cloh-ee. She answers, and I see Varrek holding a tiny creature in his arms behind her. Their baby. Varrek lightly rocks the child in his arms as he whispers something to it. Something I cannot hear. "Hello, Nalba!" she greets enthusiastically. "Everything okay over there?"

"Yes, it is fine. Cloh-ee, do you have a moment to assist me?" I ask, hoping she is not too busy with her child.

"Of course!" she replies. "Be right there."

She arrives shortly, wearing a different tunic, this one gray, whereas the previous was black.

"You changed your attire? For this?" I ask curiously.

"Oh, no," she says, waving a dismissive hand. "My milk leaked all over the other one. Then Vahla spit up on my shoulder after I fed her. Hashtag mom life."

Her words are strange, but I think I understand the context. "Yes, you are a mother," I say, my tone holding a hint of surprise that I fail to hide, "to Varrek's child."

She stops folding the pile of rags at the end of one of the tables and turns to me. "Is it weird that Varrek is mated?"

I am unsure of how to respond. I do not wish to hurt Cloh-ee's delicate human feelings, but admittedly, it is odd to think of Varrek pleasuring anyone else. "Yes," I end up telling her. "It is indeed."

"I can't even imagine. If I woke up and discovered the guy who I was fucking was married and had a kid!" she says with a bewildered tone. "I'd be all kinds of freaked out."

Cloh-ee could be a lot of things at this moment. She could be angry at the knowledge that I feel anything at all for her mate. She could be jealous that my memories of his cock are fresh in my mind. She is neither, however. Cloh-ee's voice holds curiosity and empathy. I was not expecting this, but it further solidifies why she and I have grown close since her arrival.

"It is puzzling. I did not expect Varrek to ever find his inara," I tell her, adjusting the height of the table Waldric will use for his cooking station. "And as I am not anyone's inara, I assumed the two of us would sate our bodies' needs occasionally until we both died."

"Do you miss him?" she asks, pulling out a metal box with several empty small square cubes inside.

"Do not worry, little Cloh-ee," I tell her with a chuckle. "I am not lusting after your mate. I assure you."

"Oh, honey. I'm not worried. Varrek and I share thoughts. I know how much he loves me. I see what goes through his head when he looks at me. He'd never leave me for anyone else."

"Ah, yes. The mate bond."

"But I get it," she says, looking up and meeting my gaze. "It's weird to envision someone you've been intimate with falling in love and being intimate with someone else."

That is not what plagues me. "I am more surprised that Varrek was able to find someone who would stay at his side for all of eternity."

She lets out a loud giggle with a snort at the end.

"Does he still scrunch his nose whenever he is confused?" I ask. "Does he snap his fingers repeatedly when he is trying to remember something? Or clench his jaw when he is distressed?" I could not stand the latter. The sound of his fangs gnashing against each other made me want to peel my skin off my body. It was a deeply unpleasant sound.

"Yes, he still does. I think it's cute," she says with a dreamy smile.

Varrek was not all bad. There were, of course, a few things he was quite good at. "When he fucks you, does he do that thing where he shifts his hips slightly to the left when you are about to orgasm?"

"Nalba!" she squeals in embarrassment. Her cheeks turn bright pink as she busies her hands to avoid looking at me.

I raise my hands to the ceiling. "Cloh-ee! This is something that connects us. If we can laugh about his flaws, we should be able to share the techniques that add to his sexual prowess. I remember my favorite vein on the side of his coc—"

"No fucking way, Nalba! I don't want him to know we're talking about his dick. And I don't wanna talk about his dick anyway. It's mine . . ." she adds, straightening her spine. "My dick."

I nod in agreement. "I suppose that is fair."

"Besides," she starts, "shouldn't Waldric's dick be the one we dish about?"

"Why would we do that?"

"Come on," she says, suspiciously tilting her head to the side. "You mean to tell me nothing's going on there?"

"No, there *is* something going on. Something important. He is going to cook all my meals here," I explain. "There is something in the food he makes. Taste is tied to my memories. It is the key to unlocking them. Perhaps both taste and smell," I clarify, focusing on my upcoming experiments and ignoring the thoughts of Waldric's cock that Cloh-ee encouraged. "Whatever it is, I asked him to be here to prepare my meals, and he agreed. He should return soon with his supplies, so we should tidy this area here." I gesture to the clutter along the top of the table, as well as the boxes with unfamiliar gadgets and accessories beneath.

"That's it?" she says, jerking her head back and placing a hand on her hip.

"What else would there be?"

She shrugs. "I don't know. Waldric's a great guy, though. I think he could make you happy."

Happy.

That word again.

"Cloh-ee, you have known me well since you arrived, yes?" I ask as she places each item into the box carefully.

"Yeah, I feel like we've gotten pretty close. Why?"

"Was I . . . happy? Before my injury?" I ask.

She huffs a breath through her nostrils, her lips squishing together on one side as she stares at the table. "I mean, I think so. You're a private person. You don't tell me much, but I think your work makes you happy."

"It does?" I ask. It is not necessarily a question I need answered, because, of course, my work makes me happy. This is no surprise. But her reluctance to answer reminds me of Aye-vah and Kaiva, how they were not certain of my happiness either.

"Yeah," she nods, then pauses. "Well, there's always like, five minutes of happiness when you complete a project before you pivot to 'what do I need to work on next?' and then you become consumed with that next thing, but you always take a little break to be happy."

A little break to be happy.

"I can never really tell what's going on inside your head, though," Cloh-ee adds when I say nothing in response. "So maybe you're happy all the time and no one knows but you."

Can a person be happy all the time and no one know? Not even those considered to be close friends? Does that actually occur?

Before I can dwell too much on this, Waldric bursts through the door with his arms full of bags and boxes. There must be at least five bags of varying sizes and three big boxes. He places the boxes down gently just inside the door, and the bags fall off his arms in a heap. "I am back," he says with a bright smile. "Hungry?"

There is no question whether Waldric is happy right now. He emanates unbridled joy. And he has a smile that makes you wonder if he was born with extra teeth. It is lovely.

Returning his grin, I reply, "Always."

CHAPTER 7

WALDRIC

"*Y*ou're going to cook for her? Full-time? As in, all her meals?" Elle-noor continues, asking her question in slightly different ways and following me around the food hall as I collect the ingredients and tools I need to prepare Nalba's final meal this eve.

"Yes, she wants me there preparing the food, and staying until she has finished eating it," I tell her, unable to hide my excitement. "I will be at her side for most of the day, every day, until her memories return."

"Well, that's great, bud, but who's going to cook for the clan?" she asks, crossing her arms.

"Krahn will do it," I reply easily.

His head pops up from the closest dining table where he chops raw kuhnypa meat into thin strips. "Eh? You want me to cook the entire meal this eve?"

"And the entire meals for each meal until further notice," I add. I am not worried about his sloppy knife skills, or how he sometimes undercooks the root vegetables. He will learn. This will be good for him. I have coddled him too much, I think. When he makes a mistake, I do not always take the time to show him the proper methods. Instead,

I nudge him aside and do the work for him. "You will do a splendid job!" I pat him on the back as I head to the sidewall to grab herbal mixes for tea.

He hisses a breath a moment later, and Elle-noor sighs heavily. "He just cut himself, Waldric! Are you sure this is a good idea?"

"Yes, a great idea," I mumble, not truly listening. I am too busy trying to decide what I shall prepare for Nalba's meal. It is important my selections will trigger her memories. Shall I make a spicy stew with roasted *mujitavi*? Does she like the taste of that rare fungi from Nu'Piix? Or I could grill kuhnypa strips and layer them on junasii bread with viiki spread on top.

"Waldric!" Elle-noor shouts, grabbing my attention. "We don't even know what you planned on making tonight. Can you leave us with a menu or something? At least for tomorrow's meals?"

"Certainly," I reply, deciding to go with the kuhnypa strips on bread. It is a simple enough meal I know she will like. I can concoct more elaborate meals later. Krahn holds a rag tightly wrapped around his pointer finger and uses his other hand to give me his screen pad. I pull his wounded hand toward me and check beneath the rag. "You will be fine within moments," I say to him, then lean toward Elle-noor, "we heal quickly, remember?"

She takes over cutting the rest of the meat as I note the easiest meals to prepare. I tell them to follow this same menu for three days, and I will add more options to it at that time.

"Make sure there is enough junasii bread. Have a loaf baking at all times," I tell them. "It goes with every meal. Our stock of tree fruit and berries will be enough for now. Krahn knows where to collect more. He can show you."

Elle-noor looks at my notes and lets out a whistle as her eyes widen. "Okay, I can't read any of that. Krahn, you'll need to translate. And how—"

"I am sorry, I do not have time to discuss more. I must take these things to my ma—" I slip, then quickly correct myself, "uh, Nalba. I must take this to her."

I place my hand on Elle-noor's shoulder. "Krahn knows what to do. I thank you for your help, Elle-noor. You have my gratitude."

"We're even," she says with a smile. "You covered for me when I was sneaking out to observe the tr'gorys, remember?"

I do remember. Worry tore through my gut when I realized she was stealing food to hand-feed the tr'gory pups, but she was determined to do it, and I knew she would whether I helped her or not. I chose to help her. To let her know she was not alone in her secret.

"So we are," I reply. I toss my bags over my shoulders and lift the boxes of cooking tools into my arms.

I take three steps toward Nalba's when I hear Elle-noor shout, "Wait!" as she uses her tiny legs to race after me.

"I'm sorry we didn't take the time to congratulate you before. You! At Nalba's! That's great!" she exclaims cheerfully. "Do you need any more flirting tips?"

"No," I tell her. "I am going to focus my energy on the food and let that speak for me."

She presses her lips together firmly and nods. "Genius. I love it."

We part ways, and by the time I return to Nalba's, Cloh-ee has returned, which is slightly disappointing. Although, I should not assume that I get Nalba all to myself. She is determined to focus on her projects as much as possible and will need Cloh-ee's help with that.

"I am back," I say once I enter her shop. "Hungry?"

Perhaps I am imagining it, but when she sees me, I could swear she sits up just a bit taller. She even returns my smile, which is not something that has happened before. Nalba is polite, if a bit aloof, and usually does smile when I bring her food, but this smile is different. It feels genuine, not forced. Genuine and warm.

"Always," she replies, holding my gaze.

I wait for my stomach to stir, for my vision to blur around her, for my heart to feel as if it is going to burst from my chest—any sign of the tether. How wonderful it would be in this moment to discover that Nalba is my inara, that we are fated to be together.

But I feel none of these things. Just my rapidly beating heart and sweaty palms, but those are a constant when she is near.

Nalba rises from her stool and gestures toward the table against the wall. "I thought you could cook here. The fire pit is there," she points to the end of the table, "and you can store your things on this shelf."

"Yes, this shall work well," I tell her as I pick up the boxes and place them on the shelf beneath the table.

Nalba goes back to where she was sitting before and resumes her chatter with Cloh-ee. I try to keep my focus on unpacking my things and organizing my new cooking station, but it is quite difficult knowing how close Nalba is. I could steal glances at her all day long. What a gift to be in her presence this often.

"Hang on," Cloh-ee says from behind me. "Let me pull up that list we made the other day."

"I do not understand why I refused to document my findings and list my projects," Nalba mutters. Her voice is muffled. When I glance over my shoulder, I notice her hands covering her face.

Cloh-ee 'mmm's briefly and says, "Well, it *was* something I suggested a few times, but you weren't interested in it."

"Why? Why would I refuse that?"

"I really don't know," Cloh-ee replies. "You always said you had a system that worked for you, and you didn't see the need to change it."

Guilt settles like a rock in my stomach at listening to their conversation. It is just so easy when my task does not make much noise to cover the volume of their voices. Nalba is clearly frustrated, which makes me ache. I do not like seeing her upset, and that has been her near-constant state of mind since she awoke.

"Cloh-ee," Nalba says, moving her stool aside. I can hear her footsteps as she moves around the room. "This is refuse. It is food scraps. I see no need to keep it."

"Me either." Cloh-ee laughs. "I think that's actually trash, though. You would sometimes keep a piece of bread or a clump of rice if you were testing the snack saver elixir on it, but I don't recall you testing the elixir on *pluwobs*, though."

"Snack saver?" Nalba repeats with a confused tone. "What is that?"

"That's the stuff you'd put on the travel rations to extend their shelf life," Cloh-ee explains. "It was a project that mainly benefitted the hunters at first, so they could pack food for long excursions and not worry about it going bad, but it was also really comforting to have on hand, you know? In case of an emergency or a storm that knocks out our power, it's good to have that stuff."

"I suppose you are right," Nalba replies, her tone despondent. How could she not see her own brilliance in the execution of that project? Perhaps it is Yignnuf's tinny and arrogant voice in her head, repeatedly telling her she is not good enough. I witnessed his cruelty more than once—yelling at his apprentices, shaming them in public for an experiment gone wrong. If he had laid a hand on Nalba in front of me, I would not have hesitated to watch the bones of his face crumple under my fist. But from what I witnessed, he tortured her only with words. When he died from the virus, I was elated.

Nalba, however, seemed lost. She was on her own creatively for the first time, and still felt the need to operate under Yignnuf's strict rules despite his absence. Not long after that, Varrek asked her to join our clan and leave Trovilia.

If that is all fresh in her mind, I can understand why she lacks confidence. If you were to tell the old Nalba, the Nalba that existed before her head injury, how clever she is, she would agree without hesitation. I am not so sure how this new Nalba would respond to the compliment.

I find places for all my tools, then begin laying out ingredients for Nalba's next meal. I even make extra, so I may eat with her, which is something I have not yet done.

The meals I plan to make for her are mostly original dishes using ingredients we have in abundance here on Oluura, but some are Trovilian staples I have recreated using Oluuran spices and vegetables. I am hoping the combination of new meals and familiar ones from her life on Trovilia will trigger her memories.

Cloh-ee and Nalba continue going through various items that were left out by the old Nalba, trying to determine their use. "We'll make a new list," I hear Cloh-ee say more than once when Nalba determines an item useful but unsure where it fits. "There!" Cloh-ee says after a long period of silence. "This list is really coming along. I have to get back to Varrek and Vahla, but we'll pick this up tomorrow, yeah?"

"Very well," Nalba mutters, her tone thick with disappointment.

"It's gonna be okay, girl. I promise." I turn to see Cloh-ee's arms wrapped around Nalba's shoulders, giving her a comforting pat. Cloh-ee waves good-bye to me and, suddenly, Nalba and I are alone.

I clear my throat, cutting through the heavy quiet in the room. "Your meal is almost done," I tell her.

She looks up from a small pile of miscellaneous items and shoots me a bright smile. "Lovely!"

I put the finishing touches on her plate—placing the grilled kuhnypa strips on top of the bread slathered in viiki. Adding a fresh sprig of *dohni* herb to each plate, I step back, pleased with the presentation.

I wipe off my hands and carry our plates to where Nalba sits at her table. Plopping myself on a stool across from her, I wait. She must take the first bite. I crave her approval of my dish as much as I hope the food triggers another memory. She pushes the items to the side and licks her lips as she admires her plate. "This is something I like?"

"Yes, I have made it for the clan before. I recall you enjoying it."

Nalba does not use her utensils. She picks up the meat and breaks off little pieces with her hands. When there is a particularly tough piece, she wills her claws to grow so she can swiftly slice it. "You can use these," I tell her, lifting my own eating utensils and showing her how. These are items we brought from Trovilia. It is unlikely she has forgotten how to use them.

"I know," she mumbles with a mouth full of meat. "I just wanted to try it this way."

It is peculiar, yes, but it is also . . . charming. There is viiki spread on the corner of her mouth, and the juice from the meat drips down her chin. Seeing her covered in the food I made does something to me. Something primal. Visceral. It reflects how well I am caring for her, and how much she enjoys when I do.

Everything in my body is telling me to throw these plates out the open window of her shop, tear off her leggings, and shove my face between her thighs. I want her sweet juices all over my face, just as my food is all over hers.

Since I do not know how Nalba sees me, I resist these desperate urges. Instead, I reach out, the pad of my finger swiping the viiki from the corner of her lips, and I lick it off.

Her mouth falls open as her eyes track the flick of my tongue, her pupils turning her eyes almost completely black. I hear her breath coming out in short pants.

Suddenly, she climbs onto the table on all fours, nudging the plates to the side, and puts her hands on either side of my face. Then she presses her lips to mine.

CHAPTER 8

NALBA

*W*aldric tastes divine. His lips are soft and thick, much like the rest of his body. The moment I kiss him, he freezes in place, but when I thread my fingers through his mane and graze his scalp with my claws, he groans and his movements turn frenzied, urgent. A gust of wind rips through the open window, causing bumps to form on my skin and my nipples to harden. I press myself closer to Waldric, seeking his warmth.

He kisses me hard, as if he wishes to devour me whole. Then he lifts me easily off the table and drops me into his lap with my legs straddling him. I feel his hard length growing beneath his pants, and I become desperate for the friction it will cause. I grind down on him— my cunt getting slicker by the moment.

I need him inside me. Reaching for the waist of his pants, I rub my body against him, seeking contact with every part of him.

When his hand cups my breast, I am thrown unexpectedly into the past. A blurry face and body sit beneath me, just as Waldric is now, a hand cupping my breast and gripping my back as I arch and cry out in pleasure. A memory. This is a memory!

The image is not clear enough for me to identify the owner of the lips mine are pressed against, but it is clear enough to indicate that person is not Waldric. His hair is silver and shorn close to his scalp. Throwing my head back, I see that I am in my shop, straddling the clothed cock of a male in my clan, but not the male I am with now.

Confused and a bit shaken by the image, I pull back, averting my gaze from Waldric. I am not ashamed to know I have sought out sexual pleasure from another male. Not in the slightest. As an unmated female, it is my right. What I was not expecting was the cloak of shame I feel while in the lap of this other male.

It was as if I were rushing my way through the encounter so my orgasm would arrive, and I could be done with it. I felt nothing for that male. If anything, it was mild irritation that his cock was required to make me feel good. Why could I not replicate that experience on my own? Why did I need anyone to achieve sexual release?

"Are you well?" Waldric asks, reaching up and running his thumb along my cheek. "Was it a memory?" His orange eyes search mine, concern etched on his friendly face.

Waldric does not make me feel shame. I am surprised to find that in his arms, I feel cared for. Cherished. I enjoy that feeling. The taste of him lingers on my lips, the richness of the viiki remains as well, making me crave more of what we just did.

But what irks me is why the old Nalba would seek this other male for sexual pleasure when it did not make her feel good. Was there a greater purpose in it? Did he inspire her ongoing projects in some way?

"Uh," I finally mumble. "I am fine. Just a flash of something, but I could not tell what." Clearing my throat, I rise from his lap and return to my stool on the other side. I pull my plate back in front of me and resume eating. "Tastes good."

"What . . . why did you do that?" Waldric asks, his chest still heaving. There is a bit of kuhnypa juice lingering on his lips, making them glisten in the light. His mane is a mess, the knot he tied it into almost falling out completely. I want to return to his lap and finish what we were about to start, but the ghost of humiliation interrupted us. Now he asks a worthy question I am reluctant to answer.

I focus on the meal, tearing the viiki-covered bread into smaller pieces, then stacking those pieces in a neat pile on the plate. *I could not stop myself,* I want to say. *I became so desperate for your lips that it felt like they would grant me immortality.* Instead, I say, "I wanted to," with a shrug. This feels how old Nalba would handle this particular situation, I think. Given the little I have learned about her, she seems to do what she pleases.

"I see," he says, using his fist to wipe his mouth clean. He pats down the front of his shirt and straightens his spine as if he is not sure what to do next. Guilt pumps through my blood. I should apologize for my behavior. That is the right thing to do.

I finish chewing and take a sip of water from the mug at my right. "There is, um, something I woul–"

He does not let me finish. "Does this mean if I want to kiss *you*, I can do so whenever I wish?"

"I suppose that depends," I reply with a smirk. "How often do you wish to kiss me?"

I am no fool. It is clear that Waldric is attracted to me. He must want to kiss me often.

Waldric's gaze heats, and it feels like my skin is on fire. "You will know when I kiss you."

I am surprised. This is not what I expected him to say. Tilting my head to the side, I study him as he chuckles and returns to his meal. His jaw is hard and forms a square shape. I trace the planes of it with my eyes, shifting downward. And his neck . . . it is as wide as my thigh, but there is a grace to the length of it as well. How can something be strong and also elegant? How is that combination possible?

A flash of black ink peeks out from the neck of his tunic, and I see a bit of his tattoo. It must be massive. I find I am disappointed that I cannot see the rest of it. What is the shape? How much of his body does it cover? When did he get it? I am curious about all these things.

"I feel your eyes on me, female," he says without looking up. "You have questions, yes? Ask them."

How big is your cock? May I have a taste?

"Have you always been a cook?" I ask instead. "I do not remember seeing you at the market stalls on Trovilia."

"That is because I was a warrior on Trovilia." He swallows a bite of bread and takes a sip of water. I watch, entranced by the movement of his throat as he drinks. It makes my mouth suddenly go dry. "But I enjoyed cooking more, so when Varrek asked me to join him here, I requested to become the clan's cook. His crew was strong enough without me."

"You did not enjoy the thrill of battle?"

"No," he scoffs. "I do not wish to extinguish life. I want only to nourish it. With food, I am able to do that."

I nod. Another unexpected response. I cannot pinpoint why, or where this thought originated from, but I always assumed the cooks of Trovilia were forced into the trade due to a lack of other options. I never considered it to be a sought-after skill.

But what do I know? My entire life was chosen for me the day I created an automatic lace fastener for boots as a young girl. It was after Ekoya tripped on a loose lace and nearly choked on the bread she stole from me. The design was praised by the king and became a staple on every pair of boots made.

From that moment on, I was Yignnuf's apprentice. My path was to become Trovilia's top inventor. That is what Yignnuf wanted for me. What my parents wanted for me. I do not remember if that is what *I* wanted for myself, but I assume it was.

Waldric looks at me as if challenging me to respond. His expression is tight and mildly vexed. I do not understand why.

"You have a gift," I tell him honestly. "It seems it is your true calling."

He stiffens at first, then just as quickly, his face relaxes into a slight grin. "Thank you," he says in a quiet voice. I have noticed he is always smiling. Even in repose, there is a curve to his lips that indicates he is happy. So, what is it that caused his flicker of anger just now? This male is not as easy to read as I thought.

We finish our meals, and I assist Waldric in tidying up his station. "I shall arrive in the morning with enough supplies for all three meals," he tells me. "They will be things you have eaten many times, and I hope you get more than a flash of memories."

He bows slightly just before he leaves, a gesture that is reserved for introductions with kings and queens, and even though it is utterly out of place here, I find it adorable. A flutter deep in my belly nudges me back toward his station as I picture his large form standing in this very spot mere moments ago.

Do I—

Do I miss Waldric?

No, that cannot be.

He was just here. I shall see him tomorrow. Why would I miss someone I will soon see again? What is happening to me?

CHAPTER 9

WALDRIC

As I make my way along the main path to Nalba's the next morning, I pass Elle-noor on her way to the food hall. "Ah, hello, little human friend."

"Ooh, did someone get lucky last night?" she asks with the curve of her brow.

She is quite invested in my pursuit of Nalba. I might as well be honest with her. "I did, in fact." As she gets closer and stops in front of me, I lean down and whisper, "She kissed me."

She playfully slaps me on the arm. "Well, well, well. Get it, boy!"

"How was the final meal? Did Krahn manage?"

Elle-noor makes a clicking sound on one side of her mouth. "Eh, not good. Not great. Somewhere between inedible and mediocre."

"Oh, that is . . ." I survey the heavy bags in my arms, all full of ingredients for today's meals. Nalba will not mind if I am a bit late. I should help Krahn. "Allow me to—"

"No fucking way am I going to let you bail on your dream girl just to help make breakfast." Her expression is stern and reminds me of my mother when I would get crumbs all over my furs. "Go, cook up some memories for Nalba. We've got this."

"Are you certain?" I ask, hoping she does not change her mind.

"Yes, in fact, one of the new humans was a pastry chef on Earth. Anna, I think. She offered to help Krahn with the bread, so that's something."

That is joyous news. Krahn preparing the meals on his own could easily lead to disaster. At least with someone watching him, and offering to help with part of it, he will feel less pressure. "I am pleased by this."

Elle-noor sends me on my way with a mock kick to my behind, and I enter Nalba's without knocking.

I find Cloh-ee at her side with one of the new human females facing both of them, a tortured look on her face. Her name has slipped my mind. "I would like a few more douku orbs, if you can spare them," the female says. Vye-let, I believe it is.

"I do not know what that is," Nalba replies flatly.

"They're like balloons filled with soft light, weightless and they come in several sizes," Cloh-ee explains. "I'm pretty sure you invented them not long after settling here. That's what Kaiva told me. I know how to make them. I used to help you with those all the time."

Nalba continues staring at Vye-let. "Why do you appear sad?"

Vye-let takes a step back and huffs a breath. "I'm not sad. I just . . . I don't like the dark. My room needs more light. It will help me sleep better."

"No problem! We'll get those done today," Cloh-ee promises cheerfully.

Vye-let does not thank them. She just wipes her eyes and turns on her heel. But then her eyes land on me and widen for a moment before she storms out. Strange. Do I frighten her?

"I think she's just having trouble adjusting," Cloh-ee whispers to Nalba. "She'll be fine."

Nalba ignores her and shoots me a smile. "Greetings, Waldric," she says. Unless I am imagining it, her tone is not the same as it was the day before. It has a slight rasp to it, almost like a purr when she says my name. My cock strains against my thigh, and I wonder if I should start wearing loose pants while I am here. Nalba's mere presence makes me hard. If she continues speaking to me that way, I will spill my seed where I stand. I am sure of it.

"Morrivikka, Nalba, Cloh-ee," I reply, turning toward my station, and strategically holding one of my bags in front of me to hide my obvious erection.

"Hey, Waldric," Cloh-ee says as she moves about the space, gathering items from various boxes. "Nalba, these are the medium-sized orb skins. I think these will be the right size for Violet's room."

Nalba grunts in response as they get to work. I can feel her eyes on me as I light the fire pit and begin preparing the *rihlmeal*. Flexing my back and clenching my backside, I cannot resist giving her a show. Simultaneously, I do my best to focus on the meal I am preparing. Rihlmeal is an easy dish to make in large quantities, which is precisely why I listed it as the first meal for the clan over the next three days. But what will be special about Nalba's rihlmeal is the inclusion of b'fiko syrup mixed in—giving it a boost of sweetness—and a sprinkle of ground *jibazi*.

"There!" Cloh-ee exclaims. "We just need the leathery strings to tie off the top. I think they're over there, bene—"

"Oh, it is no bother, Cloh-ee. I shall get them," Nalba offers. Her footsteps seem to synch with the beat of my heart as she crosses the room. Then I feel her backside brush against mine as she passes me. "So sorry, Waldric," she purrs. "That was completely unintentional, of course." She places a hand on my back and traces my spine with a single finger.

"Liar," I whisper.

She chuckles and leans up next to my ear. "A filthy one." Then she sinks her fangs into my earlobe. It is so sudden and unexpected that I worry I will collapse from arousal. Instead, I proceed to knock the pot of boiling water to the floor.

"Uh, my apologies," I stammer, panicked that I exposed myself as a bumbling fool. Tossing a towel onto the floor, I return the pot to its grated ledge above the fire pit and wipe up my spill.

"O fah! It is but water. There is no need for apologies," Nalba says, shooting me a wink as she returns to her seat next to Cloh-ee.

If I was concerned about the kiss we shared being a fleeting moment of desire, she has proven me wrong. She enjoys touching me. I think she finds me pleasing to look at. This is good. It means I can follow through with my plan. I will kiss her this day, and it will be such a heated kiss that she will not be able to think of anything but me. No memories will interrupt us this time.

I wish for her memories to return, just not when I have her writhing in my arms. Any other time is preferable.

"So we put this liquid inside the skin, and it creates light?" Nalba asks Cloh-ee.

Stop listening to them.

I am trying to do as my subconscious instructs, but it is impossible for my entire body to not respond when Nalba speaks. It is as if her voice alone controls me. She has the power to ignite my soul with a single word, and just as easily, she can snuff it out.

"Yup!" Cloh-ee says. "It's also safe for animals to consume, and it nourishes the soil. These are strung up all over the village, and they're probably the most environmentally friendly object in the galaxy." She lets out a proud sigh. "And *you* created them, Nalba!"

There is silence until Nalba asks, "When exactly did I create them? Do you know? And why?"

"Oh," Cloh-ee starts, "that was long before I got here, so I'm not sure. Safe to assume you guys needed a source of light and this was your solution. I can ask Varrek, though."

Nalba makes a sound of displeasure. "No, it is fine."

"Okay, well I'll just go deliver these to Violet," Cloh-ee replies. "I'll be back this afternoon once Vahla's down for a nap. Varrek will be back on daddy duty by then." Before she exits, she says good-bye to me, and the door slams shut behind her. Nalba rushes to the door and shoves the back of one of her stools beneath the door handle, essentially locking it.

She turns to face me, and her eyes swirl with heat. "Finally," she mutters as she stalks toward me.

"Your meal is almost ready," I tell her, nerves tightening my stomach. I hold up the pot of rihlmeal so she can see.

Her eyes never leave mine, though. She unwraps my fingers from the pot handle and takes it from me, setting it on the table next to the fire pit. "We can eat later."

We.

Yes, *we* can eat later. Right now, *we* can do . . . other things. Feed *other* appetites.

She wraps her arms around my neck and leaps into my arms, wrapping her legs around my waist. I turn her around and seat her in the center of my workstation. "Do you wish to kiss me now?" she asks in a husky whisper.

"Yes," I reply against her lips before taking them.

She pulls back before I can kiss her. "And here I am pouncing on *you* again. I suppose I am too impatient."

This time, she leans in, and I pull back. "You have no idea how long I have waited for you, Nalba. Never be patient with me. Pounce."

She smiles, her golden cheeks darkening slightly before our mouths collide. Her tongue swipes at my lips, and I do not refuse her entry. The moment she sucks on the tip of my tongue, my sac tightens against my body, and I almost spill my seed.

Nalba chuckles when she feels me quiver against her, then her expression turns puzzled as she looks to her left. I see that her hand is covered in the sticky, blue b'fiko syrup as she pulls it from the bowl. "What is this?" she asks as she spreads her fingers wide and then presses them together, mystified at the strings of syrup that drape from finger to finger.

"It is b'fiko syrup. Taste it. It is sweet," I tell her. Then I lean down and take her pinky into my mouth, swirling my tongue around it, and releasing it with a pop. The thick nectar slides down my throat, and as much as I am enjoying the taste of it, I wish it were the sweetness from Nalba's cunt instead. "Mmm," I groan, closing my eyes.

When I open them, I find Nalba staring at my mouth. "Hmm, it does look quite delicious," she says as she presses her thumb to my lips and traces a line of syrup along my bottom lip, all the way to the top. But she does not kiss me like I thought she would. Her tongue glides along the same path of her thumb, cleaning the syrup from my lips, slowly. "Mmm, Waldric," she says, flicking the tip of her tongue at the corner of my lips once more. "Your syrup is mouthwatering. I could guzzle it down all day long."

If she wishes to play this game, I will gladly participate. I dip two fingers in the syrup bowl until they are blue from end to claw. With my clean hand, I thread my fingers through her smooth, thick mane. Then I pull, exposing her neck. "And what if I spilled my syrup all over that sweet face?"

My pull was not hard enough to cause pain, but enough to let her know she is not in control, despite what she may think. Her eyes widen in shock at first, but then I see a flicker of hunger in them. She likes this. "What if it dripped along your throat?" I ask, painting her neck blue as I trace a line from chin to collarbone. The moment I am done painting her skin, I run my tongue back up to her chin, pressing light kisses along the way.

"I want it, Waldric," she pants. "Cover me in it." Then she says the three words I have longed to hear since I first laid eyes on her. "I am yours." Upon hearing it, I no longer act with a light touch. My primal needs surge forth, and I tear at her clothes, desperate to see her skin bare. I rip the seam of her tunic, shredding it up the side.

She does the same to mine, then her hands tug at the waist of my pants as she kisses my bare chest. "Off!" she cries out when I am still not naked. Without speaking, we let go of each other so we can quickly remove our own clothing. Once that is done, my hand flies to my chest, covering my heart as I take her in. Her body is slender and lean, her breasts bounce slightly as she straightens her spine. Her breasts are smaller than the humans', but they are big enough to fit inside my palms. Her nipples are a lovely dark brown shade, and they stiffen under my gaze.

Nalba reaches out and takes my cock in hand. Syrup still coating her hand, she strokes me once, and the grip of her hand paired with the wetness of the syrup about does me in.

"Fuck," I grit as I start to pump into her hand. Then I stop, growling at my own selfishness. "No!"

She shrinks back at the volume of my voice, and for a moment, I see genuine, palpable fear. I quickly decide this is not the ideal moment to demand the name of the person who planted this fear in her head so that I may rip their innards out in front of their weeping family.

"Nalba, I–" I stutter, "you will always come before I do."

Then I gently guide her legs apart, her cunt slightly darker in color than the rest of her glowing golden skin. Her folds glisten with her juices, causing saliva to fill my mouth. She realizes she is safe with me, and I see her visibly relax, leaning back on the table. I dip my finger in the syrup, then mark the area between her breasts with a dot. I continue creating a dotted line down the center of her body until I reach the apex of her thighs.

Using my other hand, I spread her pretty folds and inhale deeply. I would normally take this time to tell her how addicted I already am to her scent, but I cannot. I cannot speak. Nalba's cunt is wet and lovely and right in front of my face. Words would only get in the way.

Tracing the outer edges of her cunt with the syrup, I watch as her back arches slightly. Her eyes are locked on mine, and she is desperate for me. "Please, Waldric," she confirms with a keening cry.

"Mine" is all I can say as I lean in and shove my tongue inside her wet heat.

CHAPTER 10

NALBA

*M*y hips buck the moment his mouth is on me. Bracing my hands behind me on the table Waldric uses as his workstation, I lean back farther, giving him better access. Goddess, this male is lapping at my center as if it is his only source of sustenance. And I fucking love it. He continues his assault on my cunt, thrusting in and out with his tongue just as he would with his cock. Occasionally, he takes a break by licking the syrup from my folds and adding more so he can do it again. I squirm under him, surprised by how wet this sticky play is making me.

I assumed he was sexually inexperienced. Everything about him makes it seem like he does not know what to do with a naked female spread before him.

I was very, *very* wrong. As he sucks and kisses my folds, he inserts two fingers inside me. Oh yes, he is incredibly skilled. He pumps into me, groaning each time my walls clench around his fingers. "You are so wet for me, pretty one. You like how I fuck you with my hand?"

"Y-yes," I pant, gripping the edge of the table until my knuckles turn pale yellow. Each time I look down at him, my eyes are drawn to his tattoo. It covers his entire shoulder and the right side of his chest in large, black swirls. I want to trace each loop with my tongue. "More, Waldric. More!"

He adds a third finger and begins following the trail of syrup dots he left down my chest and stomach with his tongue. In and out, he thrusts his thick, calloused digits, and while I am filled, I need more. I need all of him. His cock is magnificent to look at, especially with the way there is a slight curve to it. I want it inside me, pumping and stretching me wide.

When he licks the final dot clean, he kisses his way over to my left breast and sucks on the firm tip. I am shaking all over, sweat coats my skin, and I feel as if he is nudging me toward the edge, but pulling me back each time I threaten to go over. I let out an anguished cry as his mouth leaves my breast, and he makes his way to the other. Then he grabs my mane again and tugs at the same moment his fang brushes against my nipple, and his fingers slam into me. I am gone.

He keeps his hands where they are in my mane and deep inside my cunt, but his lips cover mine to silence my screams. I ride out my release, my entire body quaking in his arms as I claw at his bare back. As I start to come down, he releases his grip on my mane, stroking it instead. "Yes, Nalba," he whispers against my mouth. "So pretty."

I press my forehead against his, still trying to catch my breath. "Where . . . Where did you learn to do that?"

He pulls back and tilts his head to the side. "Where do you think I learned it?" he says with a chuckle. Then eventually asks, "Do you want me to provide names?"

"No, no," I reply, huffing out a breath, amused. "I suppose I was not expecting that from you."

He closes his eyes and nods. "You think because I knock over a pot of water when you touch me, that I do not know how to properly work a female's cunt?"

"It was just surprising. A good surprise!" I assure him. Pressing a hand to his chest, I revel in his warmth. His skin is soft and comforting. There is give to his middle and his sides, unlike the sharply cut abdominals of the warriors. I find I prefer it. He is like a fur blanket, and I want him to cover me from head to toe, shielding me from the universe.

When I notice a drop of syrup on his hip, I reach down and scoop it with my finger and lick it off. "Another good surprise is your cooking," I tell him as I pull him close. "You are extremely skilled."

Suddenly, his features darken, and he steps out of my grasp. His cock is still hard as steel, bobbing between us and practically reaching for me. I do not understand the shift in his mood, but I am certain I can fix it. I reach out for his cock, and when he steps farther back, I hop down from the table. "Come here." When he does not, I ask, "What is it?"

He scratches the back of his head as he avoids my gaze. "I suppose I should be relieved you find my cooking skills acceptable, right?"

What? I do not understand his words. "Waldric, I—"

"Because, otherwise," he cuts me off, "what would I do with my life? I lack the intelligence to do anything else, so I would be lost."

I lower my voice to a whisper. "I do not think you would be lost." Waldric is angry with me. That much is clear. But I do not know why, so I offer a theory. "Is this because I was surprised you licked my cunt so well? I did not me—"

"No," he answers quickly. His shoulders slump and he reaches for his pants. "Just forget I said those words."

I watch him dress, confused by how quickly things fell apart between us. Once he shoves his feet into his boots, he stomps over to his workstation and quickly tidies the area but leaves the food. Using a bowl next to the pot of what I assume is cold rihlmeal, he scoops out a portion for me and drops the bowl on the table. "Here is your first meal. I shall return for the next one." He knocks over the stool wedged beneath the door handle, and the door slams shut behind him.

I am left naked, sticky, and clueless as to what I did wrong.

In a trance, I shakily put my torn tunic and leggings back on, pick up the stool, and sit down in front of my meal. I regret taking a bite of rihlmeal the moment it touches my tongue. It is a congealed lump of cold in my mouth, and I spit it back into the bowl. Looking over at the b'fiko syrup, I consider adding it to the rihlmeal, but the sight of it just makes me sad.

What happened here?

Why did Waldric flee? What did I do to cause the drastic shift in his mood?

My appetite has evaporated entirely, and Waldric's behavior has left me puzzled, and a little hurt. I must find something else to distract myself with. My feet take me in circles around the room as I go over the encounter in my mind.

Everything was fine . . . until it was not.

He had syrup on his hip, and I wiped it off. Could that have done it? Did he prefer to keep the syrup on his skin? Was he saving it for later? That seems odd, but I would not have judged him for it.

Perhaps I am pondering the wrong questions.

What would the old Nalba do in this instance? The Nalba that works among clutter and refuse. The one who creates lights from soil-nourishing liquid. The one who assumed she would not need to note her projects because they were safely cataloged inside her head.

As my gaze drifts over the shop the old Nalba spent all her time in, a beam of sunlight illuminates a large clear jug, catching my eye from where it sits beneath the table on the far wall. I approach it, and carefully remove the boxes obstructing my view.

It is a large jar containing orange liquid, in a slightly less vibrant shade than Waldric's eyes.

Twisting off the cap, I breathe in the contents of the jar and immediately begin coughing. It smells terrible. Acidic and sour and strong enough to have me breathing through my mouth. But there are several jars with the same orange liquid lined up on either side. I count at least seven. Whatever this is, the old Nalba made sure to keep an abundance on hand. But what is it, exactly?

I suppose there is only one way to find out.

Tipping the jug back, I take a swig far too large for a first taste. It burns my throat as it slides down to my belly, but it also warms my insides. It must be ale. Not very good, but ale is ale.

Then, a flash.

I see a mug in my hand, the same orange liquid sloshing over the sides of it as I wade through a crowd on the main path of the village. Darkness surrounds us, but the warm light from hundreds of douku orbs placed in the trees above gives us enough light to see. I am laughing. There is music. People are dancing.

We are celebrating something. I do not know what, but I seem to be thoroughly enjoying myself.

Then it is gone.

It is a mere fragment of a memory, but a memory, nonetheless. And the answer to my earlier question becomes clear.

The old Nalba would imbibe. And perhaps, more memories will come.

Closing my eyes, I tip my head back and swallow as much of the ale as my throat will allow.

"Beh," I mutter in disgust before taking another long pull. The sooner I begin feeling the effects of this ale, the sooner my memories will return. Right? Yes, that sounds right.

By the time Cloh-ee arrives, I do not know what time it is, but I have consumed three jars.

"Nalba," she mumbles, looking around the shop with disbelief in her large brown eyes, "what the hell is going on here?"

She looks down at my legs. "Why aren't you wearing pants?"

"Hmm?" Dropping my gaze, I discover that my leggings are, in fact, gone. When did I remove them? I cannot recall, so I decide it is unimportant. "I am sure they are somewhere, dear Cloh-ee."

"Are you drunk?" she asks as I make my way over to her via several small twirls.

The bottom hem of my tunic flares out when I twirl, and the sight is hypnotic. I continue twirling because it makes me giggly and dizzy.

"Nalba!" Cloh-ee calls again as she places her tiny hands on my arms, stopping me.

I pout at my sudden stillness. It was much more pleasant when everything was a blur around me.

Cloh-ee's face splits in two, then three Cloh-ee heads briefly before melding back into one. "Mmm, yes. I believe I am."

She shakes her head, then glances at the empty jars around the worktable she and I share. "It's the middle of the day. Where's Waldric?"

"Do not know," I answer quickly. That aggravating male just left my head. I do not wish to think of him now.

"Hey, Nalba! Just came to ch-" Aye-vah stops when she enters the shop, Kaiva at her side. "Whoa," she waves her hand in front of her nose. "It smells like a frat house in here. Looks like one too."

"What is frat house?" I ask, suddenly eager to learn more about human culture. "Did you live in a frat house, Cloh-ee?"

"Nope. Every frat house I've been to is a den of horrors," she says dryly. Then she turns to Aye-vah and Kaiva as I start humming a song I learned as a child. "Uh, yeah. So, Nalba's wasted."

"I see," Aye-vah replies with a nod. She takes three steps in my direction. "Nalba, Kaiva was hoping to get an update on your memory loss, and I was thinking you and I could try a meditation session. See if that knocks anything loose. But maybe today isn't the best day for it?"

"Well," I say before taking another sip of ale. "My memories have returned in only a few quick flashes. Single images without context. My head is still broken. That is my update."

"Ooohkay," Aye-vah replies as she makes notes on her screen pad. "And the meditation, would you like to try tomorrow?"

"Yes," I tell her. "We shall meditate tomorrow, Aye-vah." I have grown tired of being still inside my body. Time for more twirling. I am on my third spin when I hear the door open again, and familiar heavy footsteps make their way across the floor.

"What is this?" Waldric calls out, a mixture of confusion and worry in his rich voice.

When I lift my head to look at him, the room is still spinning, and I stumble. My hip slams into the corner of the nearest table and I go down, face first.

CHAPTER 11

WALDRIC

The moment Nalba starts to stumble before me, I do not hesitate—I dive. I know the path her body shall take as soon as she loses her balance, and I will not let her endure any more pain this day. As I am sliding beneath her, my arms are outstretched, and she lands inside them just in time.

Her eyes are dazed when she looks at me, but I can tell the moment her vision clears. An appreciative smile spreads across her face as she returns my embrace. But all too quickly, her memories of this morning return, and she shoves against my chest as she crawls away.

My arms remain open as I take her in. She wears only her tunic, and her mane is rumpled and frizzy, just as it looked when I left her. "Are you well?" I ask. She does not answer me. I do not know where her leggings are, or why she has chosen to spend the better part of the day guzzling Bruvix's ale, but I know I am to blame for it.

I turn back toward Cloh-ee, Aye-vah, and Kaiva. "I shall handle this. I am the cause for Nalba's current state."

"What happened?" Cloh-ee asks quietly. Her eyebrow lifts in a way that tells me she has some idea of what occurred, and she disapproves.

Looking back at Nalba, my heart fills with sorrow. I see remnants of the syrup along the side of her neck. Her eyes are bloodshot and unfocused, her feet are bare and dirty, and she shivers in just her tunic as she yanks it down to cover her legs.

"A moment of foolishness," I tell Cloh-ee without lifting my gaze from Nalba. "That is all."

Aye-vah clears her throat. "Okay then. We'll come back tomorrow."

"Get some sleep, Nalba," Cloh-ee adds as the three of them leave the shop.

The silence that fills the space between us is so loud, I almost wince. Crouching to her level, I extend my hand. "Come."

She scrutinizes my hand, then meets my eyes. "What do you want? I can find my own food. I no longer need you."

Her words feel like a slap, but I should have expected as much.

"Come," I say again. I was given the opportunity to intimately care for the female I have dreamt about for years and I ruined everything in moments. Nalba needs me. She needs what I can offer. I will give it to her, and I will expect nothing in return.

Eventually, she places her hand in mine and I help her rise to her feet. Before she lets go, she says, "The rihlmeal was revolting."

A laugh escapes me at her words. I should not find her coldness funny, but her ability to state her feelings so plainly is one of the things that drew me to her in the first place. "Well, it is meant to be eaten hot, not cold."

She shakes free of my grasp, and strides over to the far corner of the room, lifting something into her hands. Leggings. She puts them on slowly and shoots me a glare when she finds me watching. I turn around and begin cleaning my workstation. The rihlmeal, the syrup—it is all just as I left it.

"I shall make you something better," I say over my shoulder.

"I should hope so," she slurs under her breath as she sits at the table.

Emptying the bowls and pots, I put them aside knowing I will drop them at the dish station once Nalba has eaten. "It is true, there is not much worse than cold rihlmeal. I have eaten it many times when I failed to feed myself at the food hall. It made me queasy."

After a long moment, Nalba asks, "Why would you do that to yourself?" Her tone is not as curt.

"I do not need to eat first. The clan's needs are more important than my own." I pull out a deeper pot, typically used for stews, and fill it with water. As I place it over the fire pit, still burning from this morning's meal, I add, "I will enjoy the meal much more knowing their bellies are full."

We do not speak much after that. I face my station and the wall my station is pressed against, and Nalba remains quiet. Leaning into my routines, I begin to hum a familiar tune while I cook.

Once the *sinaks* are peeled and chopped, I toss them into the water, adding a pinch of *haalju*, a spice that adds flavor. Then I spin on my heel and place a mug full of water in front of Nalba. Her forehead was resting on her arms, and she jumps at the sound of the mug. "Drink," I tell her.

She bares her fangs for a moment before lifting the mug to her lips. I hear her gulping it down as I stir the sinaks. She places the empty mug down as I spin around and refill it. The look she gives me would make most males wither, but I am unfazed. I know how frustrated she will be if the ale makes her sick and bedridden tomorrow, leaving her unable to work.

"You will feel better. You know this."

Without verbal complaint, she continues to drink.

Once the sinaks are soft, I drain most of the water from the pot and begin pressing my wooden spoon into them until they turn into a whipped mass of beige. I sprinkle a bit of *groxi* flakes on top and scoop a large heap onto Nalba's plate, then my own. Then I place a handful of grilled kuhnypa cubes beside it.

She offers me a tight smile and begins eating right away.

About halfway through the meal, the quiet becomes too much. Too intense. I drop my utensil and sigh. "I must apologize for my behavior. It was unacceptable."

Nalba chews slowly as her eyes search mine. They drop to my lips, pausing there, before lifting back to my eyes. Then she looks down at her plate, her cheeks darkening. "Why did you leave?"

Because I am a coward.

"It is hard to explain."

She huffs a breath. "Try."

I was feeling too many things at once. So close to taking you exactly as I have imagined. But I still do not know how you see me. I do not know if you think I am an unintelligent failure as a male.

I open my mouth, but the words do not come. Eventually, I say, "I had a memory of my own, and it shook me."

Her face softens as if she understands. Of course, she does. "I did not realize how powerful memories could be until I lost so many of them. They are quite jarring when they arrive without warning and without context."

I grunt in agreement, not knowing if words will provide comfort.

We finish the meal in silence. Nalba lets out a yawn as I take her plate away and brew some water over the fire pit for tea. The sky is darkening outside, but she has had a . . . unique day, and it would be best if she ended it now to rest.

Handing her a mug once the tea is ready, I say, "Your body is craving sleep. Will you listen?"

She gives me a nod and a half-shrug as if accepting defeat. When she rises, her foot catches on the leg of the stool. Luckily, she reaches for the table and catches her balance. But it is enough of a sign that she is still feeling the effects of the ale, and I refuse to let her stumble another step. "Here," I say, handing her the mug. "Do not drop it." She lets out a surprised squeak as I lift her into my arms.

"I can walk," she tells me in a snide tone.

"I am aware." But I do not release her. I would carry her everywhere if she would allow it.

Climbing the steps out of her shop and toward her bedroom, I check to make sure my gait is smooth so as not to spill the contents of the mug clutched tightly in her hands. She reaches down to turn the knob once we make it to the second level of her home. Gently, I place her on top of her bed and set the mug on the table beside it.

She wiggles out of her leggings and climbs beneath the furs. "Sleep deep," I tell her as I tuck the furs beneath her delicate, pointy chin.

Turning onto her side, she faces away from me and is asleep within moments.

As I listen to the heavy breaths she lets out, and the soft snarl punctuating each one, I sit on the floor beside her, leaning back against the bed. "For so many reasons, Nalba, I do not feel worthy of your smiles, your touch," I whisper, knowing she cannot hear me. "You may not be my inara in title, but you are all that the word represents. I do not need the tether to tell me that you are meant to be mine. I choose you anyway. I shall never be the fool I was this day. I shall never walk away from you again. I swear it."

Slouching down a bit until the back of my head hits the bed, I let go of my shame, my guilt. Tomorrow is a new day.

It is not long before I surrender to the darkness of the room, and sleep pulls me under.

CHAPTER 12

NALBA

*T*he dry scratchiness of my throat wakes me. Desperately fumbling for a beverage of any kind to soothe this ache in the darkness of my bedroom, I find a mug on the table next to my bed. It is tea, and it has chilled while I slept, but it is enough. Despite the lack of heat required to fully enjoy it, the familiar sweetness and fruit flavor of the tea shoots me back in time.

I am sitting in my shop, surrounded by gleaming blades and the smell of leather. There is a mug to my right with a faint curl of steam rising off the top. I drop the wide leather band onto the table and take a sip. It is tea. This tea.

There is a sense of pride, a sense of completion that has me sitting taller on my stool. I wrap the band around my wrist, securing it in place. Then I dip my middle finger through the thin loop that rests inside my palm. A small, devastatingly sharp blade emerges from a hidden compartment, and once it is out, I take it in my other hand and hurl it across the room. It lands in the center of my target—a block of wood from a rotting Ga'Nvi tree nailed to the wall—with a muted thud. "And it is done," I say to no one.

Then the memory evaporates like mist on the wind. But it was enough. It was a full, rich memory. It made sense to me. I completed a new kind of weapon—on my own—and tested it successfully in my shop.

"It is working," I mutter, looking down at the mug in my hands. My memories are returning.

Out of the corner of my eye, I notice a large boot lying on its side, and when I lean over the edge of my bed, I find its owner.

Waldric.

He is sprawled out on his back, his large hands resting on his stomach with his head turned to the side. His lush lips are parted, and dribble escapes the corner of his mouth like a leaky spigot. I find myself in awe of him—the strong line of his jaw, the broadness of his shoulders, and how much space he occupies at any given time. Such an imposing size, but with a tender heart beating in his chest.

Could the tether form between us someday soon? For many, it does not happen at first sight, so it is possible that is in our future. But do I want an eternal mate? Another person constantly in my space? And inside my head? I do not know how old Nalba would answer the question, but new Nalba would not hate the idea.

"Hello, hello!" I hear Cloh-ee call from downstairs.

Waldric stirs and scrubs a hand down his face as his eyes slowly blink open. "Eh?"

"Cloh-ee has arrived," I tell him as I climb out of bed, putting my pants on.

He looks around the room with a furrowed brow. "I wanted to stay in case you needed anything, but I did not intend to spend the night. Apologies," he mutters, his voice a low rasp that makes my core heat.

"I did not mind your presence," I tell him honestly.

Waldric shoves his feet into his boots and follows me down the staircase that wraps around the tree and leads into the shop. "Greetings, Cloh-ee," I say through a yawn.

"Sorry to show up so early," she mutters as she digs through a box beneath our main worktable. "Vahla had me up at the ass crack of dawn for a feeding and I couldn't get back to sleep. Plus, Varrek needs to train today. He's getting restless around the house." Then she looks up and realizes Waldric is here as well. "So, I thought . . . I would . . . take the, um . . ." she clears her throat, failing to hide her smirk at the two of us looking disheveled and exhausted, "take the afternoon off."

"That will be fine," I reply, ignoring her stares. "I know what we will work on this day."

"Uh, I will go check on Krahn," Waldric says as he reties his mane into a tight knot. "I shall return later for first meal."

Just as the door closes, Cloh-ee is at my side and gripping my hand. "Did I interrupt something?"

"Unfortunately not, tiny human," I say, poking the tip of her strangely soft nose. "He fell asleep on the floor."

Cloh-ee frowns at this. "Aw, man! I was hoping for some juicy deets."

I stare at her, trying to understand her words. "You are hungry?"

She giggles, the sound light and lilting. "No."

We take our seats at the table, and I fill her in on the memory that came to me earlier.

"The armbands! Yes, I have one of my own!"

"This is a weapon *you* use?" I ask, surprised. I cannot envision this tiny creature hurting a *xugutt* fly without shedding a tear.

She smiles brightly. "Thank you. People underestimating me really adds to the overall satisfaction of landing a blade in my target. Whether it's the rotten wood in Varrek's training room, or the throat of my enemy."

Just when I think I know Cloh-ee, she reveals another delightful layer of herself I was not expecting. I can see why the old Nalba enjoyed her company.

"What other weapons have I created?" I ask. "Was I working on any before my head injury? Does Varrek request the design and I create it based on his specifications? Or do I plan the entire design myself?" I do not know what the immediate needs of the clan are in terms of inventions that will make their lives easier, but I do know Varrek is the kind of male who will constantly fret over his people's safety, and if there was a battle recently—which apparently there was—he must want to replenish that stockpile.

"I'm like, ninety-nine percent certain you made them yourself without any input or oversight from Varrek."

Yes, that sounds like me. "Do we need more after the battle?"

"I think we're okay for now," she says. "I know Bzzsil Chi had more weapons on his ship that the guys were able to steal before Niro torched it."

"Nee-roh?"

"Oh yeah, that's Kate's mate. He's a dragon. Erm, draxilio, actually."

Draxilio? Those mythical creatures that would shift into massive-winged creatures with spikes down their backs and fire in their lungs? "This is a human? Mated to a . . . draxilio?" I cannot picture it. They are terrifying, monstrous beings.

"Yep!" Cloh-ee exclaims cheerfully, failing to notice the concern in my tone. "They live in Niro's caves not far from here. Sometimes they stay at the house they built here in the village, but mostly they're at the caves. And she's pregnant!"

That gets me to my feet. "Your human friend is carrying a fire-breathing draxilio inside her stomach?"

"Nalba, calm down," she says, lifting her arms as if I am a fearful little creature in the forest about to flee. "It's half-draxilio, half-human, and Kate's fine. Kaiva checks on her regularly, and Niro dotes on her. He and Bruvix are even good friends now."

Bruvix? Good friends?

These words do not make sense together. But I suppose if a constantly scowling, miserable male like Bruvix is to become anyone's friend, it is fitting it is with the deadliest known creature in the galaxy.

The world is so different from how I remember it. Thinking about the enormous pile of information I do not know, I plop down on my stool with a sigh. Then my frustration from a lack of release when Waldric left me covered in syrup resurfaces. "Tell me, Cloh-ee. What do you do when you wish to orgasm without Varrek?"

"Without Varrek? Do you mean masturbation?" Blood rushes to her cheeks at the word.

"Yes."

"Well, I'm not comfortable showing you, but I could explain ho—"

"Cloh-ee," I say, laughing hard now. "I do not need instructions on how to pleasure myself. I was wondering more if there was anything you use when you do."

"Oh! Like, toys?"

Now she understands. "Yes."

Cloh-ee's shoulders drop and she looks visibly relieved. "Truthfully, I haven't felt the urge for solo play since I got here. Varrek and I have sex three or four times a–" She pauses, giving me an awkward smile. "Sorry, is that weird?"

"Of course not. I have no remaining interest in Varrek. Please speak freely."

"Okay cool. So anyway, I'm not opposed to it, and I'm sure Varrek would love to watch, or even join in, but I haven't lately. Plus, it's not like my vibrator is here, so that takes some of the fun out of it."

Hmm. "What is this?"

"It's a sex toy. Did you guys not have those on Trovilia?"

"Of course, we did," I reply. Some of the finest toys in the galaxy. The *noogatohro* was a personal favorite of mine. "I did not bring any here, however, and I am in need of one."

"Girl, never leave home without your sex toys!" she shouts, giving me a sly grin. "My vibrator was amazing. I'm so glad I'm mated to the real-like version of it."

"What does that mean?"

"You know," she lowers her voice to a whisper, "because they vibrate."

She speaks as if she is sharing a secret. I know our males' cocks vibrate. Then a very sad thought occurs to me. "Do human males not vibrate?"

"Nope!"

I am aghast. "Then . . . what do they do?"

"I mean, they're very similar. They just don't vibrate."

I suppose with the right amount of skill and friction, a cock that remains still would work. But what I am picturing has me baffled.

Grabbing my screen pad, I decide to sketch out the *noogatohro*.

This conversation is too intriguing to let fizzle. After I explain the way it is used, Cloh-ee rises and stomps her foot. "You have two clits? Seriously! You lucky bitch!"

Her words would sound angry if she were not also laughing. "I did not realize human females had only one."

She looks closer at the drawing of the noogatohro, pointing at the long, cylindrical shape, leading to a round, bulbous head. Looking at the slight curve of it, and the vein I added along the side, it looks more like Waldric's cock than a standard noogatohro, but I say none of that to Cloh-ee.

She asks about the mechanical suction heads, and I tell her that they emerge later for added stimulation of our k'billita. I explain how the cylinder vibrates the moment it is inserted, and the suction heads gently work our k'billita with pressure that steadily increases as soon as it registers that our cunt is wet.

"Our clits are only on the outside though," she says, "unlike yours, so this thing wouldn't really work for humans." Then she draws a version of her toy, showing me where the "baht-ur-eez" are kept.

"O fah, those would not be needed here," I say as I dig out the solar charged *kahzo* packs I could attach to the exterior instead.

"Wait, so are you saying you could make vibrators for us?" she asks, excitement in her voice.

It was not my original intention, but she is practically bouncing with anticipation. "Why, yes. Of course, I could." I shall make an improved version of a noogatohro as well. And I know precisely whose cock to model it after.

CHAPTER 13

WALDRIC

*K*rahn is not doing well. The line at the food hall is longer than I have ever seen it. I can feel restlessness from the clan as I pass them. Elle-noor is not here, I realize. It is just Krahn and Ann-ah, and they are frantically moving around each other by the fire pits in a way that makes it seem as if nothing is ready.

"Krahn, I would like to che–"

"We are aware, Waldric!" he snaps. Ann-ah hastily pulls a loaf of junasii bread from the fire pit, shoves it into a basket as she squeals about burning her finger, then pours the fresh dough into the pan before throwing it back on the open flames.

I walk around the pits, looking at what they have, and move to stand behind them. "I am happy to give you space and let you finish this, but if you would like some help, I am offering it."

Krahn grunts as he stirs the pot of rihlmeal. "I should not require your help. I can manage this on my own, just as you have done."

He is a proud male, and I can see he is frustrated. I do not blame him. He has never managed the food hall on his own for more than a single meal at a time. I have left him to run it for entire days now. It is no wonder he is struggling. Stepping closer to his side, I say quietly, "It takes time to do all of this." I survey the line again, and it looks as if at least four more people have arrived, and I am no longer sure it is enough food. "The clan is growing, and we need to make more food. We may need more cooks."

That gets Krahn's attention.

"Truly?"

I nod. "We have added six human females to the clan, and I made no adjustments in the recipes for it." I was so anxious about Nalba's condition the moment she hit her head, and then so thrilled with the chance to help her recover her memories, that my mind has been elsewhere—specifically with Nalba.

He stares at me with hope in his light blue eyes.

"I am to blame for your struggles, friend," I say, patting him on the shoulder. "Allow me to assist you now, and I shall make the proper adjustments to the recipes before I leave."

Krahn nods, his expression filled with gratitude. I take my place in between him and Ann-ah and begin cutting the various tree fruits into thick slices. I must say, it is nice to have Ann-ah's aid. The junasii bread is something I would often forget about as I was busy preparing the main dishes. Not having to worry if it has burned is quite pleasant.

Once the tables in the food hall are filled and the line has dwindled to a few late-risers, the three of us get a chance to breathe.

"I thank you for the help," Krahn says.

"I am pleased you accepted my offer," I reply. Then I look over to the bread station and find Ann-ah fiddling with a stout metal cup as she tries to attach it to a wide metal tray. "What do you have there?"

"Hmm? Oh!" she exclaims when she realizes I was speaking to her. "I'm trying to figure out how to make muffins. You have so much dough here and only one recipe on how to make it. I figured it would be fun to try a few variations."

"Splendid. I am always eager to try new recipes," I say.

"Yeah, and if I can nail this one down," she says, using adhesive to keep the cup connected to the tray, "I can probably figure out how to whip up some kind of frosting alternative to make cupcakes." She looks up and her eyes go wide. "But don't tell any of the humans yet. I don't want to get their hopes up."

Ann-ah is seemingly as upbeat as she is ambitious, and that is impressive considering she was told she would never be able to return to her home planet not long ago.

I leave her to her tinkering as I make the necessary adjustments to the recipes based on head count and send it to Krahn's screen pad once I am finished.

"I thank you, brother," he says as I finish tidying around the fire pits and head back toward my home.

I share a modest two-level house with Lahkzo, located two homes to the left of Varrek and Cloh-ee's. As he is often away on hunting trips, it feels like it is mine alone. When I enter, I find him coming down the steps with a mug in hand. "Ah, you have returned."

"Mmm," he agrees. He is a male of few words.

"I must wash before departing once again," I tell him apologetically, though I am sure he would prefer to have the place to himself.

He grunts in response and begins filling his mug with water from the spigot. As quickly as possible, I cleanse myself in the wash box, change into a fresh tunic and pants, and I am back out the door.

As I make my way toward Nalba's to prepare her morning meal, I run into Bruvix and Elle-noor with Stahn-lee trotting along at her side. "Hey, Waldric, what's the latest?" Elle-noor asks as she scratches behind Stahn-lee's ear. The tr'gory pup is growing so large, she barely has to reach down to pet him. He is almost as tall as she is, which is not very tall at all. On the other side of her, Bruvix takes me in with a nod, his face forming its usual scowl.

"Well, Nalba drank three jars of ale yesterday morning, and I put her to bed before the sun set behind the trees," I tell them.

"Oh no!" Elle-noor gasps as Bruvix replies, "Which ale?"

"I do not know," I answer him. Then I realize they had just left Varrek's home. "Were you speaking to Varrek?"

"Yeah, Queen Ekoya called," she replies. "I think he's still talking to her."

Ah. "I must go," I tell them. Once inside, I race toward Varrek's training room, and there I find him with a screen pad in his hand and the Queen of Trovilia on the screen.

"Is that Waldric I see?" she asks when she notices my presence.

Trying to catch my breath from racing up the stairs, I mutter, "It is. Apologies for my interruption, but if you have the time, Queen Ekoya, I would like to speak with you."

"Certainly," she says with a knowing grin as Varrek hands me the screen pad and exits the room. "Glad you are here because I have been hoping to speak with you as well."

CHAPTER 14

NALBA

*L*ater that morning, Waldric bursts through the door to my shop just as Cloh-ee and I have finished smoothing out the molds for our toys. "Greetings!" he says once inside, putting ingredients down on his workstation. I notice his long mane is down and still slightly damp. It falls in wavy black tendrils down his back, and my fingers twitch with the urge to play with it. "What have you there?" he asks, taking a peek at the long golden rods in our hands and giving me a puzzled look.

"Oh, just silly feminine things," Cloh-ee replies quickly with a dismissive wave. "You know, for that time of the month."

"I am afraid I do not know. Silly feminine things?" Waldric repeats as he starts placing ingredients on the chopping block in the center of the table for this morning's meal. "How do they work?"

"Damn, that's usually enough to deter human men from asking any follow-up questions," Cloh-ee says under her breath. "Forgot who I was dealing with."

She pinches the edges of the mold together on the bottom and uses her thumb to smooth any remaining creases. "Oh, um, little of this, little of that," she mumbles as she gets to her feet in a hurry. "Well, I've gotta go feed Vahla, but I'll be back after Varrek gets home from his morning training session." Cloh-ee takes one final, adoring glance at her vibrator before rushing out the door.

Waldric peers at the door then turns to me with his brow furrowed. "That was an odd reaction from Cloh-ee, was it not?"

I grunt in response. "She is human. Everything they do is odd."

He chuckles, the sound rich and lovely. "This is true."

Then I focus all my attention on completing my mold. Cloh-ee and I used a pliable clay alternative called *gavneyah* that I perfected under Yignnuf's tutelage. It requires no more than half a day's time to set once it is molded. I showed her how to shape it around the base structure that holds the small mechanical vibration case that will deliver the same delicious quiver that Trovilian cocks have. Once the larger mold is complete, I work on the suction head attachments I will add later.

Waldric and I continue working, him on the meal he is preparing, and me on my mold. It is quiet but . . . a comfortable lack of sound. Occasionally, he will hum or whistle as he begins a repetitive task, like dicing or stirring, but he stops the moment he needs to focus. His back flexes beneath his tunic with each movement, and my mind begins to wander. I picture the two of us mating in various positions and places around my shop, my claws scraping along his neck and chest, following the path of his tattoo, and my fangs sinking into the skin of his shoulder, his soft belly, and all over that strong back of his.

"Done!" he calls out as he serves our meals.

"Uh, splendid." I quickly shake my head free of the spell I was under and move the molds Cloh-ee and I made to the window. Then I rinse my hands beneath the spigot and join Waldric at the table.

"This is junasii bread with sliced tree fruit, lightly grilled, with savory viiki spread between," he says, pointing at each item.

It smells of nature and spice and the warm comfort only freshly baked bread can illicit. A moan escapes me the moment I lift the bread to my lips and take a bite.

Waldric watches me closely, his tongue trailing along his bottom lip as I swallow. I remember the feel of that tongue on my cunt, the girth of it filling me in the most sinful way. I find I want nothing more than to leap over this table and seat myself on his face, but would he welcome that kind of behavior?

"Never be patient with me. Pounce." His words play in my mind, and I place my utensil on the plate. But then, shame fills my gut at the memory of him rejecting my touch and pulling away from me. I do not know if Old Nalba ever experienced rejection here on Oluura, but I know I certainly did not while on Trovilia. It felt brand new when Waldric did it the other day. I am not eager to feel that way again. It made me feel exposed and insignificant.

Then there is the way he cared for me the previous eve. The way he carried me to bed and remained by my side in case I needed him in my drunken stupor.

The two vastly different versions of Waldric leave my head spinning.

But what am I expected to do? Wait until he gives me some sign that my embrace would be welcomed? Wait for *him* to embrace me? Who has that kind of patience?

"Anything coming back to you?" he asks, breaking through my thoughts.

"Hmm?" Oh, he means memories. "No. Nothing," I reply. Nothing from before I hit my head, anyway. *The memory of your claws digging into my flesh as I rubbed myself against you is quite clear, however.* "I did recall completing the design of the armbands with throwing knives, though," I offer instead. "Did I tell you this? It came back to me while drinking the tea you made."

"That is wonderful, Nalba!" His smile is so wide, it looks like it hurts his face. It is then that I realize how supportive Waldric has been through this entire ordeal. He truly wants my memories to return, perhaps more than I do. But why? Is there something he has not shared with me? Was he close with Old Nalba?

"Waldric," I start, "what were we like before my head injury?"

"You and I?" he asks, his voice suddenly timid. I nod, and he clears his throat. "Uh, we were . . ." he trails off.

His reluctance to continue makes me nervous. "Were we enemies?"

He laughs. "No, not at all."

"Then what?"

"We . . ." he sighs, dropping his utensil on the table with a clatter. "We were not close. We were just two members of Varrek's clan, nothing more, nothing less."

That does not make sense to me. The attraction I feel for him now, the joy I experience in his company—was I completely unaware of it all?

"It is fine," he says, his tone soft. He lifts his utensil and presses the edge of it into the bread, cutting it into smaller pieces. "You did not pay much attention to me."

I scoff. "O fah. That is ludicrous." He must be lying now. Trying to trick me with a silly fable.

He takes my hand in his. "But I paid attention to you, Nalba. Whenever you entered a room, I could look nowhere else."

My gaze drops to his lips, and I feel my heartbeat quicken.

"Greetings, Nalba, Waldric!" Kaiva says as she and Aye-vah enter the shop.

I realize then that I stopped breathing while Waldric spoke, and I let out a series of coughs to catch my breath. "Hello," I eventually reply. Still shaken by his words, I stare at my mostly untouched meal.

Aye-vah's eyes dart between Waldric and me as if she can sense the heat between us. "Still good to do your evaluation today?"

"Certainly," I say, tugging at the neck of my tunic for some air. "But let us conduct this in the med room, yes?" I am certain I would not be able to focus if we remained here with Waldric stealing sly glances at me, especially with what he just revealed. "I am going to eat while you check my head," I tell Kaiva as I grab my plate and follow them out the door.

"I shall return later," I call out to Waldric.

He nods. His gaze is heavy-lidded, his orange eyes swirling with desire. Later cannot come soon enough.

Inside the med room, I hop up onto one of the beds in the center of the room and continue eating my bread and fruit as Kaiva takes my mane down and examines the wound on my scalp. Once I am finished eating, I put my plate on the tray beside the bed and I follow Kaiva to the med tube. "This will tell us how much the swelling in your brain has decreased."

"Very well," I reply as I lie back inside the cramped, sterile tube. These machines do not bother me. The healers of Trovilia have been using them for as long as I can remember. I am used to shutting my eyes, ignoring the strange beeps, and letting my mind wander to my projects as I wait for the tube to reopen.

"There were go," Aye-vah says with a smile as she helps me climb out. I hop back onto the bed and fix my mane into a tight knot while Aye-vah and Kaiva review my scans.

"So, how are your memories, Nalba?" Aye-vah asks as she steps in front of me. "Anything coming back?"

"Yes," I reply proudly. "There have been a few memories, and the most recent one was more than just a flash. The entire memory played out in my head. It had to do with the knife armbands I created. Cloh-ee helped me with additional information when I told her about it."

"That's great! Please feel free to ask any of us to fill in the blanks for you when your memories come back," Aye-vah says. She places a hand on my shoulder and gives me a light squeeze. "We're here for you."

"I thank you," I tell her.

Then Kaiva steps forward, holding her screen pad against her chest. "Your swelling has gone down significantly. I am quite pleased with the way this scan looks." She shows it to me, but, like last time, I just see various throbbing shapes.

"Okay! Wanna try a mediation?" Aye-vah asks, clapping her hands together. "It might uncover some more memories of yours."

"Yes," I reply. Meditation is a common practice on Trovilia, and I am familiar with its mental and emotional benefits. Unfortunately, Waldric's words are still echoing in my head, and I worry I will not be able to focus on anything else.

She climbs onto the edge of the bed, and we sit cross-legged facing each other. Following her instructions, I focus on my breath and loosen each muscle she names as she begins from my head, all the way down to my toes.

Aye-vah's voice takes on a soothing, yet authoritative tone as she continues guiding me. She tells me to envision a flower opening wide as I breathe out, and closing tightly when I breathe in. It helps keep my thoughts about Waldric at bay, if only temporarily, as I picture the flower instead of his face. Or his strong back. Or the way he nods to himself after he takes the first bite of food and is satisfied with the taste.

O fah, I am doing it again.

"Now, imagine letting it all go," Aye-vah instructs, "the tension in your jaw, your fingers—the areas you don't often notice that carry the most stress."

I blow out a long exhale as I try to release my clenched fists.

"Aye-vah!" Kaiva calls out, panic and awe warring in her voice. "Come look at this!"

Aye-vah gives me an apologetic smile as she rushes to Kaiva's side. It is just as well because the meditation was not working to uncover my memories anyway. I watch as Kaiva swipes through several pictures of colorful blobs on her screen pad, noting the changes to Aye-vah.

They look engrossed in whatever this is and will probably be busy for some time. I rise to stand, and just as I take a step toward the door, I hear Aye-vah ask, "So what does this mean?"

Kaiva sighs, her breath shaky, and replies, "The humans seem to be . . . changing."

CHAPTER 15

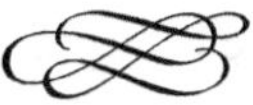

NALBA

"Changing how?" I ask, interrupting Aye-vah and Kaiva's discussion. This so-called change in the humans clearly has nothing to do with me, but my curiosity has been piqued.

Kaiva frantically swipes through the images again, her head shaking. "Aye-vah, please send a comm to Varrek, Cloh-ee, Ahlvo, Bruvix, and Elle-noor. Tell them to come here so I may share my findings."

"What about the new girls?" she asks Kaiva as she reaches for her screen pad.

Kaiva pauses, her gaze going unfocused. "No, we will not alert them yet."

Within moments, the rest of the group arrives, including Waldric. "You came too?" I ask as I stand beside him at the back of the room.

He wipes his hands on the rag draped over his shoulder and shrugs. "Cloh-ee grew very concerned when Aye-vah told her to rush over here, knowing you were still getting evaluated. She suggested I come as well."

I am glad Cloh-ee urged him to come along. Whatever announcement Kaiva is about to make has nothing to do with my injury, but I have no doubt the news will be shocking, and I find comfort in his nearness.

"Okay," Aye-vah begins as we all circle around her and Kaiva. "Kaiva has been looking over the data from our blood and cell scans, comparing it to when Kate, Chloe, and I first arrived, to the most recent work-ups."

Kaiva steps forward and clears her throat. "I have also looked at the initial cellular work-ups of the new humans and compared those to yours as well."

"Wait, where's Kate? She should be here too," Cloh-ee says, looking around as she holds a sleeping Vahla in her arms. I have not yet laid my eyes on Cloh-ee and Varrek's child, but I find myself longing to see her face. To see how the child of a human and Trovilian looks. There is even part of me that wishes to hold her.

"They are at the caves," Bruvix replies. "I shall send a comm to Nee-roh so they may listen." Once Bruvix reaches them, he holds up his screen pad facing Kaiva, so the two can listen in.

"The cells of Cloh-ee, Aye-vah, Kay-teh, and Elle-noor have changed significantly since they first arrived," Kaiva continues. "At first, I thought the change was only in Cloh-ee and Kay-teh, and as Cloh-ee was recently with child, and Kay-teh is currently, I dismissed the changes being related to pregnancy. But looking over Elle-noor's and Aye-vah's as well, I can see a clear correlation between when the cells began to change, and for all four of you, it is when you completed the mate bond."

"Ah, the power of alien sperm," I hear Kay-teh mutter from the screen pad in Bruvix's hands. The rest of the humans giggle in response. "Changing how though? Are my boobs going to get bigger?"

I have not met this human or her mate yet, but I have heard stories about her odd sense of humor.

Kaiva chuckles and turns her screen pad in our direction, showing us the colorful blobs. "Nothing like that, Kay-teh. What I think is happening, but I cannot be certain of this just yet," she pauses, "is that the aging process humans naturally go through is slowing for you."

She quickly swipes through several screens until landing on a screen that is split into four quadrants. "This is Cloh-ee's data from her first days on Oluura. Notice the rate at which her cells would shift."

The images Kaiva is showing us do indicate a change. The cells are slightly different colors and shapes. There is also some shading in the center that appears to grow.

She swipes to the next screen, which is a single image. "This is after she completed the mate bond with Varrek." And the next screen, showing another quadrant. "These are her cells after the mate bond, but during the same length of time as before it. Look at how they differ."

Kaiva is right. The cells in each of the four quadrants look exactly the same, whereas the cells in the first image look slightly different in each quadrant. It appears as if her cells have frozen in time.

"They are no longer aging, then?" I ask.

"That is my theory," Kaiva says, nodding. "Perhaps with the inter-species mingling of blood and seed, the humans will live longer than is typical for their race."

"Well, that's a relief," Cloh-ee says with a sigh, pressing a kiss to Vahla's forehead. "I've always hated the idea of Varrek living to two hundred and me dying at eighty."

Kaiva audibly swallows, her gaze dropping back to her screen pad. "There is something else." She pulls up another screen with eight quadrants. These cells look very different from Cloh-ee's. "These are Varrek's cellular changes. His cells seem to be aging quicker than normal, and they began accelerating after the mate bond."

"You are saying Cloh-ee and I will die together," Varrek says, a hint of elation in his voice that shocks me as he gazes down at his mate, and then his daughter. "We are now aging together, at the same rate."

"Yes, my son," Kaiva replies, her tone solemn. "I will have to do several more tests and monitor all of you more closely in order to confirm these findings, but that is what I think is happening."

The sadness in her voice makes sense to me. His happiness at this news does not. He is going to live a shorter life simply because he mated a human? How tragic. "That is quite unfortunate," I whisper to Waldric. "Can you imagine?"

His lips purse, then he gazes down at me thoughtfully. "I could imagine. I do not find it unfortunate in the slightest. It is beautiful knowing you will not live even a moment without the person you would die for."

I am learning that Waldric is an unwavering optimist. It is a nice sentiment, certainly, but discovering your life will be cut short because of your chosen mate is not something I could so readily accept.

The syncing of cells to align age between mates is a common occurrence among Trovilians, but as we all typically live two centuries, it is not such a dramatic diagnosis to receive. Trovilian mates will either lose or gain a few years in order to die when their mate does. But between Trovilians and humans, the gap is much more significant. Will Varrek lose a hundred years of his life because Cloh-ee is so very fragile? Or will Cloh-ee gain a hundred by being mated to Varrek?

Out of the corner of my eye, I watch as Elle-noor leans into Bruvix. He wraps his arms around her and presses a kiss against her mane. It seems they are fine with this outcome as well.

Puzzling.

"What about me?" Kay-teh hollers. "You said my cells changed too? Even though Niro isn't Trovilian?"

"Ah, yes, Kay-teh," Kaiva says, her focus returning to the screen pad in her hands. She swipes through several images before turning it around to face us once again. "These are your cells. They have indeed changed, but not in the same way the others have. I do not think your aging process has halted." She presses her fingers together and then spreads them apart across the screen, making the image in the third and fourth quadrants bigger. "Yours are starting to look like Nee-roh's, as if your cells are transitioning into a draxilio."

Well, that is interesting.

"Now, I am not suggesting that you will soon be able to fly and breathe fire, Kay-teh," Kaiva quickly clarifies. "This could be a direct result of the pregnancy. But as you are the only human on Oluura mated to a draxilio, I would like to start collecting regular samples to gain a better understanding of what is happening."

"Uh, okay," I hear Kay-teh reply. "It'd be cool to breathe fire someday, though. So, if there's any way to make that happen, I'm down. But maybe after the baby is born."

Kaiva chuckles at Kay-teh's strange request. "Nee-roh, I have also noticed something fascinating with your cells since you became mated."

"That is?" he asks, his tone stiff and haughty.

"Have you noticed any changes while in your other form?" Kaiva asks.

Kay-teh replies for him. "Yeah!" she exclaims, turning to address her mate. "You said you felt stronger the last time you shifted. And remember the other day when you could breathe fire right before the shift?"

Nee-roh clears his throat. "Yes, this is all true."

"Ah," Kaiva says, triumphantly. "That is what I suspected. The cells here appear more vibrant, healthier. The data reflects that. I am not surprised you are experiencing increased strength in your other form. But I would also like to monitor you more closely as you are the only draxilio we have frequent contact with."

"I do not see the need," he replies. "Contributing parts of my body, even on a microscopic, cellular level makes me uncomfortable. No." His face exits the screen, and I see Kay-teh take his place in a huff.

"Don't worry," she adds. "He gets a little perturbed with stuff like this because of his upbringing, but I'll work on him."

"Is that everything, then?" Aye-vah asks Kaiva after a brief pause, noticing the sudden restlessness in the room.

"Yes, that is all," Kaiva says, closing her screen pad. "Please continue to see me at least once every five days to give your sample. I shall provide updates on my research as they come."

"And you don't want us to tell the other humans?" Cloh-ee asks.

"No!" Kaiva quickly replies. "Do not tell the rest of the clan, either. Not yet. I do not know how they will react to learning that mating with humans slows the human aging process, and speeds the Trovilian aging process, simultaneously. There are males who are desperately hoping the tether forms with one of the humans, and I cannot foresee this information causing anything but distress."

As the group starts to disperse, I make my way over to Cloh-ee and

Varrek. Words come out of my mouth that I do not expect. "May I hold the little one?"

Cloh-ee and Varrek exchange a glance that indicates they are equally shocked by my request. "Sure," Cloh-ee eventually says, cradling Vahla's head as she places her in my arms.

The first thing I notice about the child is how small she is. Much smaller than a Trovilian baby, but since this baby is part-human, I suppose it makes sense. "She is named after your mother, yes?" I ask Varrek without lifting my head. I am far too distracted by Vahla's pale golden skin and the tuft of brown hair with a small patch of silver by her tiny, pointed ear to look elsewhere.

"Yes," Varrek replies. I can hear the smile in his voice.

"A beautiful tribute," I add. Varrek's mother was truly a magnificent female. She would have loved to meet Cloh-ee, and the adorable namesake I hold in my arms.

I thought the sense of longing I felt earlier would cease once I held Vahla, but if anything, it has grown. I have never felt comfortable in the presence of children, of any age, so this surprises me.

Unless Old Nalba wanted children of her own. Perhaps this feeling is an inkling of a memory, something that exists in my mind I simply cannot reach.

Cloh-ee must sense my confusion. "You're good with her," she says with a chuckle.

"I thank you," I reply, quickly handing the child back to her mother. The longing has left me frazzled, and I do not know what to do with it.

Cloh-ee hands Vahla over to Varrek, who seems to glow with pride the moment his daughter is in his arms. "You know," Cloh-ee begins, "you and Jo were lifesavers during the birth. God, that was such a scary day."

The name she utters is not familiar, but instead of clarifying that, I am stuck on the part where I assisted in a birth. "I helped you?"

"Yes! Well, you and all the girls—Jo, Kate, Ava, Kaiva, Eleanor too! You were all so supportive and wonderful," she says with a sigh. "I could not have done it without you."

What was I doing assisting in a birth? This is not my area of expertise.

"Well, I am going to take this one back home," Varrek says as he gazes lovingly at Vahla. He bends down to kiss Cloh-ee's forehead, and when he leaves, I notice that everyone else has also gone.

Cloh-ee, Waldric, and I walk together back to my shop in a heavy silence. Me, from the unsettling emotions that stirred inside me while holding Vahla, and them, from the shocking theory Kaiva presented. I decide I cannot take it anymore, and say, "Is this better for the humans than the Trovilians? The slower aging process?" I am not directly asking Cloh-ee, but more presenting it to the group. "You will live longer once you are mated to a Trovilian. That is certainly appealing, is it not?"

Cloh-ee huffs out a breath. "I don't even know where to begin with that. Because it's still just a theory. How will my cells continue to change? What other changes will occur? Will my skin eventually turn gold? Will Varrek's skin turn pasty white? Pfft, who the fuck knows!"

Her questions are valid. Though that last one paints an amusing image. "Varrek with your translucent, delicate skin? With his silver mane? He would look ill. Just . . . terrible."

Cloh-ee takes no offense to this. She just laughs. "I'd love him no matter what he looked like, but I see what you mean."

She walks ahead the rest of the way to my door and spins on her heel. "Can we not dwell on this bizarre fountain of youth thing? Because I have good news for you, lady." She swings the door open and guides me over to our shared worktable.

"Do you?" I ask.

"I do indeed."

CHAPTER 16

NALBA

"What is this?" I ask as Cloh-ee, Waldric, and I stand in the middle of my shop. Cloh-ee swipes at the screen pad in her hands. It looks like a list of some kind. It must be in her Earth language because I can read none of it.

"I was able to get Varrek to tell me everything he knew about the weapons you were working on before your head injury," she says, adding a scribble to it. "These are my notes."

"Fantastic! Can you read it to me?"

Cloh-ee's notes are rambling and somewhat vague, though that could have easily been the way Varrek described my projects. He is prone to rambling.

The majority of projects on the list are concepts in the early stages, and Cloh-ee was not able to connect them with anything she remembers me tinkering with before the battle. Except for one. The idea is an explosive that operates as a handheld device set off manually and detonating on impact. "Like a grenade," she says. She draws one, but it does not look like anything I have seen before.

This kind of weapon is not new among our kind. The innovative tweak I had come up with, apparently, was an attached heat scanner that would guide the path of the explosive to a previously specified location. "I would program the target location into the scanner, and upon release of the explosive by the user, the bomb would continue through the air en route to a certain part of the body on the intended target, yes?"

"Um, yeah," Cloh-ee says. "I think so. I remember you saying something about it landing on a target's neck, sticking to the skin, then blowing off their head. Or sticking to the target's chest in order to guarantee the most damage done to the heart. Something like that. You thought it could be useful to protect Ekoya with the assassination attempts she's been dealing with. We should call it a sticky bomb!"

That stops me in my tracks. "Wait, Ekoya? Someone tried to assassinate my sister?"

Cloh-ee clenches her teeth as if ashamed she revealed a secret. "Yeah, Ekoya told Varrek that some of the older males who were loyal to his father as king are still peeved about having a female in charge."

How very archaic. Though, I am not surprised to learn that King Muryk's pitiful followers are still holding tight to their prejudices. It is the only thing they have ever excelled at. That insidious mindset is part of why we left Trovilia and came here.

"Should I be worried about her? Is she in immediate danger?" Images of Ekoya being murdered in her castle fill my mind, and my hands begin to shake. "I should send her a comm. Or Varrek . . . yes, Varrek needs to send some of the crew to Trovilia. To protect her."

"Nalba," Waldric wraps his arm around my middle and as soon as I register his warmth, I sink back into him, letting him take all my weight. He guides me over to the stool next to Cloh-ee and sits me upon it. Then he steps away briefly before returning with water.

"Drink."

I do as he says.

Once the mug is empty, he says, "Now breathe."

Cloh-ee takes my hands in hers and squeezes. "Ekoya is safe, I promise you. She has her own crew of warriors, and she has Cruvo. Those assassination attempts were nowhere near close calls. They were epic failures, in fact. I bet those morons knew that before Ekoya's men killed them. Their hearts stopped beating as they suffocated under a cloak of shame." Cloh-ee smiles, her expression filled with warmth, despite the vicious words she just spoke. "Feel better now?"

"I do," I say honestly, returning her grin. Despite her delicate human body, Cloh-ee's heart has the strength of a thousand waterfalls. She can tap into a level of brutality that resonates with me. Especially when it comes to keeping Ekoya safe. "I truly do."

"Good. Now, let's get back to work, shall we?" she says, showing me her sketches of this *sticky bomb* as she guides me through her notes once again.

"It does sound effective. Also, quite savage . . . no?" Though, knowing Ekoya's crew will use this to defend her, I wonder if there is something we can add to make it more so.

Cloh-ee tilts her head to the side and gives me an indecipherable look. "I've said that to you before. Your response would always be, 'If we do not create it, our enemies will. And they will use it against us.'"

Her impression of me is depressingly accurate, but she is right. Or I suppose I am right since I am the one who said it.

We spend the next several minutes looking through boxes for weapon components. The fact that Old Nalba shoved explosives into boxes with food scraps and various tools rattles me to the bone. Who is she? Why did she do such reckless things?

We put everything we find in a pile at our worktable, and I begin putting them in order of when they will be needed during the assembly stage. Cloh-ee makes her scribbles as I move things around and begin fastening them together. My hands move of their own accord as if I have done this thousands of times. I do not know how much time passes, but suddenly, Waldric is walking over with two plates of food, and my stomach growls at the sight.

"I did not want to interrupt your work, but it is time for middle meal," he says sheepishly.

"Shit! Totally lost track of time," Cloh-ee exclaims. "Gotta get back to Varrek and the little bub. See you tomorrow!" She rushes out the door, waving as she goes.

Rinsing my hands, I join Waldric at our usual meal table in the center of the room. "Well," I say with a smile, "this is the first time since my injury that I feel I have a worthy accomplishment. I was beginning to wonder if my drive would ever return to me."

"You? Without drive?" he asks in mock disgust. "You are not Nalba without it. It is not as if you did not have it, you just did not know how to channel it, or what to channel it on."

This is true. I have not enjoyed wasting my days since I awoke. It has been frustrating, not knowing where anything is or how I spend my time. All that has been made easier, though, with Waldric's help. His food has helped trigger my memories, but that is not the only reason I enjoy having him nearby.

It is his spirit, as well. The generosity that flows freely from his soul. I also appreciate the other side of him—the side I am sure not many have ever seen. The way he looks at me when he thinks I do not notice, as if he is a predator that has finally spotted his prey. I am growing addicted to his presence in my home.

"What?" he asks, giving me a suspicious glance.

"Nothing," I reply coyly, dipping my finger into the warm bowl of bright crimsons, greens, and yellows. It is a stew-like dish called *bvatee* made by mixing boiled crop vegetables and mashing them together. "You have something here," I say, pointing to my cheek.

He wipes his face and looks down at his clean hands, puzzled. It is then that I flick the glob of bvatee at him.

He grunts when it lands in the center of his forehead.

I cannot help but laugh at how ridiculous he looks with a steaming red dot on his face.

The look he gives me at first makes me shrink back in my stool. But then it transforms into something else. Something wickedly mischievous.

"You best run, pretty one," he growls. "I will show you no mercy."

CHAPTER 17

WALDRIC

How foolish of Nalba to think she can best me in a food battle. Does she think I am unpracticed in this area? A former warrior who is now a cook?

She squeals giddily the moment I tell her to run and jumps off her stool with her bowl in hand. I duck down behind the table as she rushes behind the table across the room, beneath the open window. I hear her snickering as she pokes her head up, and it is then that I fire.

"Argh," she grunts as a large glob of yellow strikes her cheek. "Waldric!"

She does not peek around her table for several more minutes. "This is no battle if one side remains hidden!" I remind her from my crouched position. She does not respond, so I pop my head up just enough to get a view of her table.

"Psst," a whisper sounds from my right, then lukewarm bvatee lands on me, covering my eyes. It is still warm, and the scents of herbs and spices I added to the dish waft into my nose.

Nalba's laughter fills the room as she scurries away. "You will never catch me!"

Scraping away the mush, I fling it onto the floor as I seek my target. Little green blobs cling to my eyelashes as I scan the room, and then I find her. Her shoulders shake as she laughs quietly from behind the tall shelving unit that sits perpendicular to the row of tables. I see her peeking through the area between the shelf and the box beneath it, and I duck before she can follow my path.

Rolling a ball of red into my palm, I wait for her to stick her head around the shelf and release my weapon. I hear it hit her neck with a slapping sound and I move closer as she frantically wipes it off.

Never letting her leave my sight, I strike her again with the bvatee, this time hitting her stomach in a yellow splatter.

"That is it!" she screams, and for a moment, I worry she has grown tired of our game. Then she is grabbing large globs in each fist and hurling them one after another. She misses the first two but lands the next three—letting out a triumphant bellow at the sight—and soon I am returning her fire with the same ferocity, landing my throws on her knee, her hand, and her chest.

"Come closer, pretty one!" I yell, hoping to lure her away from the safety of the shelf. "How courageous could you be if you continue hiding behind that big thing?"

"Using the shelf as a barrier does not make me fearful," she hollers back. "It shows I am smarter than you for finding it first!"

There is no denying that.

Then I spot Nalba crawling along the floor behind the shelf and peeking around the other side. She darts around the other side, and as she's crawling back toward the far table, I hit her in the calf with a clump of green.

"Ah!" she cries out, clutching her leg as if in pain. "Cramp! My leg is cramping. Waldric, do something!"

There is such agony in her voice that I drop my bowl and rush to her side. "How can I help?" I ask, looking over her small frame in a panic. "Shall I massage it?"

Slowly, her mouth stretches into a satisfied grin as she reaches up and swipes a red blob across the tip of my nose. "I win."

I chuckle at her smugness. "You do not play fair."

She stretches her body and casually puts her bvatee-covered hands behind her head. "I do not seek recognition for honor. I merely seek victory."

"And victory you claimed," I tell her, offering my hand. She takes it, and I pull us both to our feet. Nalba takes a step closer, her longing gaze focused on my lips. Another step, and our hands are still clasped as she traps them between our bodies.

We are both covered in bvatee—our clothes, our manes, and every exposed speck of skin. Yet, I have never found her more breathtaking.

The side of her mouth curls up slightly as she drops my hand and brushes a loose strand from my mane off my cheek. Just as she wraps her arms around my neck, closing the space between us, the clump of bvatee that was covering my nose falls, landing on her chin with a *glop*.

It ruins the moment.

We both laugh as we look down at ourselves, then around the room at the mess we have made. "I am going to wash," she says.

"Ah, yes," I reply, looking toward the door. "I shoul–"

"No," she says, interjecting. Her cheeks flush. "Stay. You can use the wash box after me."

"I, uh, suppose I could," I reply. Her request catches me off guard. Though I do have a change of clothes stashed away among my tools. I am a careful cook, but even I am not immune to spills and stains. And after our syrup play the previous day, I must remain prepared to get messy. "Then I shall clean up around here until you are done."

She smiles at me as she saunters toward the stairs that lead up to the second level where her bedroom and washroom are located. Tossing a towel over her shoulder, I catch it and begin wiping the food off my face and neck. Once the largest chunks of bvatee are gone, I rinse the towel beneath the spigot, wring out the excess water, and start scrubbing away the mess.

And what a mess we made.

The food battle could not have lasted more than a handful of minutes, and in that time, we covered her shop with bvatee. It is impressive.

By the time Nalba descends the stairs, wearing only a tunic, I have just finished wiping the tables. I was about to begin on the floors and shelving unit, but her long, muscular legs are bare, her shiny, black mane is wet, and her skin glows like the sun.

"It is fine," she tells me as she takes the towel from my hand. "I shall take over from here." Her eyes sparkle with need, and her smile steals the breath from my lungs. "Go wash."

"Very well," I mumble, distracted by her beauty. Although, when am I not? "Uh, I am going to . . ." I trail off as I pull my clothes from a bag between two of the metal boxes at my workstation. "I shall return." I wave awkwardly as I pass by her.

She chuckles, though I can tell it is amusement and not mockery. The washroom is a cloud of hot steam as I enter. Stripping my clothes off, I let out a sigh as the thick mist of the room hits my skin. The wash box is a tight fit. It accommodates my height, but I cannot turn around without one or both of my shoulders brushing against the sides.

Ah, well. It will get the job done.

Images of Nalba flood my mind as I scrub away the hardening crust-like patches of our meal.

She almost kissed me.

If the bvatee had not fallen off my nose at the worst possible moment, would we be a tangled heap of limbs rolling around on the floor of her shop? Would I be deep inside her body right now, filling her sweet cunt just the way she likes?

Or would she have stopped it from going further than a kiss?

Worse, would I have been the one to stop it?

My hand finds my cock as I imagine her supple, lean body pressed against mine.

Using the soap she has in a small bottle in the corner of the wash box, I lather my hand and stroke up and down my length.

I recall the way her body shook as I licked along her pretty folds coated in b'fiko syrup, and the thrust of my tongue inside her tight, wet cunt. Her soft lips parted in a silent scream. The way her thick thighs squeezed the sides of my head.

Groaning, I press my forehead against the wall as hot water runs down my neck and my backside. I tighten my grip as I stroke up and over the head before jerking my hand back down. Picking up the pace, I continue to fuck my hand—my hips bucking as the memory of Nalba's nectar floods my tongue.

Her name leaves my lips in a growl as I jerk my length faster, harder. I see the anguished look on Nalba's face as she got closer to the edge. She let out a cry when I replaced my tongue with my fingers and rose to kiss her lips. She thought I was done with her. How wrong she was.

I still feel her thick mane wrapped around my fingers as I tugged, letting her know I had her. That she could let go of the control she constantly seeks and let me care for her the way she needs.

When my fingers spread inside her cunt and brushed against her k'billita, she spasmed all around me. Remembering the moment she came, covering my hand with her juices—that is what pushes me over.

I press my fist against my mouth as I roar into it, spraying my release all over the walls. It is then that I realize how little the tether matters. It can appear or not. That will not change how I feel.

Nalba is mine.

CHAPTER 18

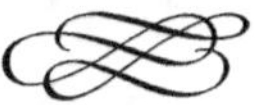

NALBA

I cannot contain the giggle that rises in my throat as I wipe up the remaining bvatee from the floors of my shop. It is everywhere. I am certain years will pass and I will continue to discover little patches of bvatee caked onto boxes and beneath shelves. It was great fun, I must admit—chasing Waldric around the room as if we were children, throwing colorful mush at each other.

Perhaps this is why I found my shop in such disarray when I awoke. Had Old Nalba just participated in a food battle?

I suppose it is not impossible, but I highly doubt it. That mess was not like this mess. That mess was mostly made up of refuse that had not been discarded, dust covering the surfaces, and food that, at one time, was fresh and colorful, but had faded into a drab gray. It was a sad mess.

This? This is a happy mess.

Waldric actually believed he could best me in a food battle. Why? Because he handles food all day long? What a silly male he is.

And beautiful . . . in a rugged, yet soft kind of way.

I should have kissed him. His lips were *right there*.

A knock sounds at the door, busting through my thoughts of

Waldric's perfect mouth. Could it be Cloh-ee back for more work? No, she said she would not return this day.

When I open the door, it is not Cloh-ee. Or anyone I recognize from the clan. This face is long, angular, and unfamiliar. Then I notice his mane. Short and silver.

Him.

The male I rubbed my body against in the flash of memory I had the first time I kissed Waldric.

What is he doing here?

"Nalba," he greets in a slightly bored tone. He passes me, entering my shop, and begins undressing immediately.

"What are you doing?" I demand, sneaking a glance at the stairs, hoping Waldric is still in the washroom. "Who are you?"

His shirt is off, revealing his lean, chiseled chest and stomach muscles. He holds the shirt in his hands, tilting his head to the side. "Are you joking with me?"

Thoroughly annoyed with having to explain this again, I summarize in a rush, "I was thrown against a tree and hit my head and now I have lost five years of memories. I remember nothing from my time here. I do not know who you are or what you are doing here, but I ask that you please put your tunic back on."

"Ah," he replies, stunned. "Many apologies on your current predicament, Nalba. That is not ideal."

I cross my arms over my chest and wait for him to answer my questions.

He seems to notice my impatience and tugs his shirt back on. "I am Lahkzo, hunter for the clan. I have been away for many days and did not know about your injury. Apologies for the miscommunication." He strides toward the door, but I stop him.

"Wait! Why did you come here?"

He turns, shooting me an arrogant grin over his shoulder. "When I return from a hunting excursion, we mate. Typically, we continue mating until I leave again."

Oh. "We are pleasure mates, then?" I did not even consider that I might be somewhat . . . entangled with another male.

"I suppose so," he says with a casual shrug. "We have never discussed what we are to each other."

His gaze holds no affection. His body language does not indicate any strong feelings toward me. If anything, he looks put out by the continued conversation. This is my pleasure mate? Him?

"Tell me, Lahkzo," I say, crossing my arms over my chest. "Do you enjoy mating with me? Is that all we do together?"

His mouth forms a flat line.

"Please," I beg. "I am trying to understand what my life has been like since arriving on Oluura. Your answers will help me."

He looks annoyed but mildly sympathetic. "Our mating is adequate, I would say. It is good enough, which is why we continue mating. I suspect it is more of a release than anything else—for both of us. And yes, that is all we do together," he says with a sigh, "I leave as soon as we both come."

The shame I felt in my memory makes sense to me now. The arrangement Lahkzo and I had fits the definition of a pleasure mating, but at the lowest possible level—a continued sexual pairing—nothing more. It does not appear as if we were even friends or that Lahkzo likes me at all.

I hear the door to the wash box close from upstairs, which means Waldric will be down soon. I must get this strange male out of here.

"Well, I thank you for your interest in being my pleasure mate," I begin, gesturing toward the front door. I do not wish to hurt his feelings by sending him away, but the neutral expression he holds would make it seem as if hurting him is not possible. "But I have taken a strong liking to another male and would like to see if the tether soon forms."

"You think this other male is your eternal mate?" he asks, incredulous at the suggestion.

Gritting my teeth, I offer a tight smile. *I will not be cruel,* I vow to myself. *I will not be cruel.* "I do not know for certain, but it feels like he could be."

Lahkzo laughs. "You are not built for an eternal mate, Nalba. Trust me on this."

The time for kindness is over. I do not like his words or the snide tone of his voice when he says them. "Your face is completely foreign to me. You did not know I was injured in battle. Why would I trust anything you say?"

He stares at me, blinking several times. "Because nothing will ever be more important to you than your work. It is all you care about. Anything else just gets in your way. You said this to me, Nalba. Many times."

I do not want to believe him. His words strike me in the chest, making me want to curl into a tight ball on the floor. But there is something there. A sense of truth.

"You sought me out because I was never in the way, and I never could be because you did not care about me." He must see the pain in my eyes because he takes pity on me and gently pats my arm. It is slightly uncomfortable, but not unwelcome. "You wish to understand the life you lived here? You did not care about anyone or anything that was not made in this shop. That is how you wanted your life to remain. Forever."

My eyes burn with unshed tears, and I scrub a hand down my face in an attempt to hide them from Lahkzo. Being vulnerable with him feels entirely wrong. It should be Waldric, and I know just how Waldric would respond. He would wrap me in his thick muscular arms, and he would promise me that all will be well.

Sadly, Lahkzo's description of Old Nalba feels right. No one here truly seems to know me, if I am happy, or how I spend my time. Not even those closest to me. Except for Lahkzo. Perhaps that was an intentional choice Old Nalba made—only let the male who fucks you without feelings see the real you.

"I shall go," he finally says. "When your memories return, and you are you again, come see me." I listen to him give me directions to where he lives, trying to keep my knees from buckling.

I do not say good-bye before shutting the door. Though, I doubt Lahkzo even noticed.

Could he be right about me? About my ambitions? When my memories return, or if they return, will I see Waldric as an obstacle in my way? Will I be so consumed with my projects that I will no longer have time for food battles with him? Will that seem like a ridiculous, childish activity?

I lean my back against the door, letting these questions settle like heavy anchors in my mind. Old Nalba has been a bit of a mystery to me thus far. Now that I am getting to know her, I do not know how to feel. Was she happiest in her shop? Is that why she did not want any distractions? Because there was no greater satisfaction than getting to create in a space that was not strictly managed like Yignnuf's facility?

Apart from the food battle, I have enjoyed keeping the shop tidy, and not because of Yignnuf's obsession with cleanliness that is ingrained in my skull. Absently, I reach a hand over my shoulder and feel the scars on my back through my tunic. The wounds have long since healed, but the memories are fresh. A messy station earned you one lashing. Not laughing at his jokes earned you two. Not agreeing with Yignnuf earned you three. Wasting supplies—four. I never earned more than three at a time. I do not know what the more severe infractions led to.

Maybe Old Nalba grew tired of tidying her shop after a long day of work. That could be a testament to how focused she was on her projects. How committed she was to making the clan's lives easier. It is noble, really.

Perhaps I should stop ignoring the signs that tell me who Old Nalba was. I should stop judging her so harshly because she seems unrecognizable, and just allow myself to become her.

CHAPTER 19

WALDRIC

Nalba is quiet when I rejoin her downstairs after cleaning myself from the food battle. Too quiet. It is not the typical lack of noise from her being absorbed in a project. It is not even the kind of quiet that means she is deep inside her mind trying to figure out how to tweak a product or fix something to make it work. Those are light, pleasant silences.

This one feels heavy. There is a crease in her brow that will not go away as she scrubs the side of her shelving unit. She does not even notice my presence until I stand beside her.

"Oh, greetings," she mutters distantly before returning her gaze to the remnants of red bvatee on the wooden slat.

"What is this?" I say, brushing my finger along her brow in an attempt to smooth the crease.

"It is nothing," she replies. She is quick to push away my concern, and that makes my worry intensify.

What could have happened while I was in the wash box to drastically change her mood? Does she regret the food battle we had? Does she now see it a silly waste of time? Or worse . . . could she have heard me calling out her name as I stroked myself in the wash box? Is she disgusted by it?

I grab a nearby towel and start scrubbing the floors, hoping this is all in my head, and Nalba is merely focused on returning her shop to a state of tidiness. We do not speak as we continue cleaning. For a time, I hum an old battle song I learned as a warrior in training. She does not seem to notice.

When I finally finish cleaning the floors, I look up to find her in the same place, scrubbing the same spot as when I arrived.

I am not imagining it then.

"Nalba, that area is clean," I tell her as I look over her shoulder. She has scrubbed the spot so thoroughly with cleaning solution that it is beginning to lighten the color of the wood. "You can stop." The neck of her tunic dips down slightly in the back, and I notice a thin silver line peeking out from between her shoulder blades. Clearly a scar. But from what? I trace the edge of it with my finger. "What happened here?"

She does not answer my question. She just turns, slowly, giving me a dazed look. It is as if she has woken from an ominous dream, and I do not know that my presence is helping. I wish she would tell me what is bothering her.

"How can I fix it?" I drop my voice to a whisper and entwine my fingers with hers. "Tell me."

"Tell you what?" she replies with an exasperated sigh, pulling out of my grasp. "I am fine, Waldric."

I do not believe her words. She is not "fine," but I cannot force her to open herself to me if she wishes to keep her heart closed. Perhaps she has grown accustomed to being alone in her shop, and my lingering presence is draining her energy. She has always highly valued her solitude—especially when it makes for a more conducive environment for her to work on her inventions.

I am happy to give her time to be alone if that is what she needs. "Krahn could use some assistance at the food hall, I am sure. I shall return for final meal," I tell her as I drop the towel by the door and step outside.

Nalba is a very serious creature, and she requires things to be a certain way in order for her brilliance to be optimized, but really, her main goal is to help others. She wishes to make the lives of her people easier, safer, and better. Many consider her to be difficult, but I do not. She knows what she needs, and often, she does not hesitate to clearly state those needs. Which makes it all the more puzzling that she was not honest with me just now.

I ponder possible theories for this as I arrive at the food hall to find Krahn and Ann-ah laughing as they take small bites of something that is clearly too hot to eat. They wave their hands in front of their open mouths in an effort to soothe their pain.

Then I notice something else—there is no line of people waiting to be served. There are a few of the elders milling about and finishing their meals at the tables, but Elle-noor is hard at work scrubbing the dishes, and the areas around the fire pits are surprisingly clean. "I see you finished early?"

"Yup! We prepped early and had everything ready to serve by the time people arrived." Ann-ah says enthusiastically before handing me a baked treat wrapped in petal paper. "Give that a taste for me, would ya?"

"What is it?" I ask, unwrapping the delicate paper we make out of flattened flower petals and sniffing it. It smells of spice powder and sweetness and dense batter. Saliva fills my mouth as I sink my fangs into the thick center.

"It's a muffin!" Ann-ah exclaims with a little hop of excitement. "Well, more of a space muffin, actually, since I didn't use most of the ingredients I normally would on Earth. I finally nailed down the measurements and I think people will like it."

Warm syrup floods my tongue and I jerk back, surprised. "Mmm!"

Ann-ah notices my expression and nods with wide eyes. "Right? The b'fiko syrup in the center just melts in your mouth. Good right?"

I finish chewing and examine the muh-finn. It has a rounded, crust-like top that is coated in large *jehli* flakes. The bottom is softer but just as rich. And in the center, Ann-ah has added a significant amount of b'fiko syrup, keeping it contained inside the muh-finn as a flavorful surprise for when one bites into it.

I am speechless.

"The clan will not like it," I say flatly. Ann-ah's face falls and her shoulders droop. "They will love it!"

Her smile widens comically, and she pumps her fists in the air as if she has just won a hard-fought race. "Oh, yay!"

"Waldric."

I spin on my heel to find Varrek standing behind me with a jovial-looking Vye-let by his side. She is a fascinating female to behold, this human. Her mane is dark at the top like Cloh-ee's but fades into a light yellow at the tips. And unlike Cloh-ee's curls, Vye-let's mane is as straight as an arrow. She is the tallest of the human females, but her head still only reaches the middle of my chest. Her frame is similar to Kay-teh's, in that it is round and shapely everywhere I look, just with a vertical advantage.

Each time I have seen her since she arrived here, she has looked miserable and sleep deprived. Today, however, her chin is lifted, and her expression is far less troubled.

"Have you met Vye-let yet?" he asks, gesturing to her.

"Not officially, no." I drop my gaze to hers and bow my head. "An honor, Vye-let."

"This is the human I told you about," Varrek says. "Remember? After you spoke with Queen Ekoya."

"Ah, yes," I reply. I do remember that conversation because it raised more than a few questions.

"Really looking forward to our trip," she says, leaning in and placing her small hand on my forearm.

"As am I, Vye-let."

The contact stuns me, but more than that, the feelings of guilt and mild disgust that come with it are the most surprising of all. It is not the first time a female has touched me, but looking at Vye-let's long, tanned fingers makes me realize there is only one female's hands I want on my skin.

Nalba's.

"I must leave now," I mutter, gently extracting Vye-let's hand from my arm. Before I know it, I am running toward Nalba's shop at full speed. It does not take me long to reach my destination, and when I do, I find it empty.

That is, until a low, breathy moan catches my ear from the back of the room, behind the tall shelving unit. I step lightly around the center shop tables, carefully avoiding the stools that almost block my path. Then I see her.

Nalba's back is pressed against the lowest shelf, and through the narrow opening between the shelf and the box beneath it, I can tell that her chest is heaving with her toes flexed in front of her as she sits on the ground.

"More, Waldric. More!" she cries out, causing me to stop in my tracks. It is me she sees when she touches herself. *Me*.

There is no greater gift than hearing my name on her lips. I am the most fortunate male who lives.

I step around the unit, and the sight before me stops my heart. Nalba is seated on the floor, her bare legs spread wide. One hand is above her head, gripping the edge of the shelf so hard that her claws dig into it. The other thrusts a long, golden item—cylindrical in shape, wide in girth—deep into her cunt as her fangs sink into her bottom lip.

Lowering myself to a crouched position, I move in front of her, between her feet, and call out to her. "Nalba, I am here."

Her eyes fly open and her hand stills.

CHAPTER 20

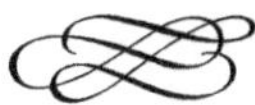

NALBA

aldric's orange eyes dart between mine as he edges closer to me. I widen my legs, making space for his big body. I am not embarrassed to pleasure myself in front of another. I have done it many times with previous pleasure mates, as toys are used between partners as a welcome addition, a third member in the encounter to ensure everyone's satisfaction. The mortification that pumps through my blood is due to Waldric seeing me on the edge of an orgasm with the help of a handmade noogatohro modeled after his cock. Can he tell I used him as inspiration for the design?

Oh, and he probably heard me say his name a moment ago when I was picturing him sucking on my nipples as he fucked me on the floor.

This is not what I was expecting when I checked the status of the noogatohro mold and discovered it was ready for use. I was alone. I was distressed by Lahkzo's visit and his description of Old Nalba. I needed a distraction.

"Do not stop," Waldric commands, his voice a husky rasp. His hands flex at his sides as if he is using every scrap of willpower inside his body to keep from touching me.

The last thing I want is for him to hold back.

Pulling the vibrating noogatohro from my core, I hold it out to him.

His eyes widen, and there's a question there. He wants my consent. I nod, giving it to him. He wraps his lips around the noogatohro, sucking my juices off it. It is an obscene sight, seeing him suck on a cock-shaped item that is an exact replica of his, but it makes my core clench so tightly, I shall never forget it.

"Let me," he growls, moving closer until his knees brush against my inner thighs. Then he takes the noogatohro in his hand and strokes the tip through my folds, getting it wet again. The moment the toy registers my come, it vibrates, sending a jolt through my cunt and up my spine.

I moan, wrapping my legs around Waldric's hips, pulling him closer.

He takes the noogatohro and rests it against my opening, teasing me. Slowly—so slowly I could kill him—he enters me, sinking the toy deeper inside my body. I reach my other hand up so that both are bracing against the shelf, and I roll my hips to meet his thrusts with the noogatohro.

"That is it, pretty one," he encourages me, using the claw on the end of his pointer finger to slice the front of my tunic in half. He does it so lightly, I do not even feel it. He parts the torn halves of my shirt, and groans once my breasts are exposed. "I must taste you, Nalba. I cannot wait any longer."

Dipping his head, he licks my nipple until it pebbles against his tongue. "Your skin is a flavor too lovely to compare. It is you . . . and I shall never get enough." He moves to the other breast, giving it the same attention as he continues fucking me with the toy. I feel the suction heads emerge inside my cunt, and I pinch my eyes shut as they begin to ripple against my k'billita. "Yes," I hiss, accidentally knocking a metal box off the shelf behind me with my clenched fist.

"Nalba," Waldric whispers as he continues flicking his wicked tongue against my breast. "My Nalba."

"Yours," I grit, every muscle inside my body starts to tighten. I am reaching the edge, leaning over the steep drop.

It is when Waldric's mouth moves slightly to the left and his fangs sink into the underside of my breast that I am thrown over. A primal bellow rips from my throat. My back arches and my feet kick up in the air as wave after wave hits me. I ride it out as my vision blurs. I feel Waldric wrap his strong arm around my back, holding me in place.

I am spent. My body is so drained of energy that I can do nothing but sink toward the floor, letting my languid limbs spread around me. Waldric is not satisfied with this, though, because quickly I am being hauled into his arms and he is carrying me up the steps toward my bedroom.

The brief trek outdoors between levels sends a shiver down my back, and bumps appear on every speck of my skin. The cold season is most certainly here. "I will keep you warm, pretty one," he whispers into my ear—*not just for tonight*, I hear in the subtext of his vow, *but for the rest of time.*

I find I am eager to experience his warmth in my bed on a regular basis.

He ushers me inside my room, pulls back the top fur, and gently sets me down. I watch as he places the noogatohro on the table beside my bed and begins removing his clothes.

"It is modeled after you," I tell him, surprised to feel blood rush to my cheeks at the admission. "Your cock."

His eyes leave my body and return to the toy. "My cock?" He stares at it a little longer, then I see a flash of recognition, probably at the curve of it. "Ah, I can see it. Yes."

"I hope you do not mind," I say. When did I become so desperate for his validation?

He scoffs. "As if I would ever be bothered by such a thing." Then he stills and shoots a proud grin my way. "I am honored, Nalba. Extremely honored."

I chuckle at his response, relief settling my insides.

A growl fills the room as Waldric's eyes lock onto my breasts, and the bite he left. "Need you." The words are filled with anguish and lustful desperation. "Do not deny me."

"Never," I reply, tugging at the waist of his pants as he removes the remaining scraps of his shirt. His swollen cock bobs in the air between us as his pants hit the floor. Pre-come glistens at the tip, and my mouth waters. What does he taste like?

Reaching out, I wrap my fingers around his cock. He is so large here that my fingers do not completely encircle him, and my inner walls clench at the thought of him stretching my insides with it.

He growls, running his fingers through my mane. Then he digs them in deep and pulls. "I do not want to come in your hand, Nalba. Not this time." He pauses. "Right now, I need to be inside you."

Without saying anything, I push back on the bed and lift my legs, wrapping my hands around the backs of my knees. "Then what are you waiting for? Fuck me."

His eyes sparkle with hunger as he takes in my spread folds, my cunt on full display. Then he prowls forward until his cock is pressed against my entrance. I nod when he shoots me a questioning glance, and he pushes forward. Slowly, he continues until he is fully seated inside me. It burns at first, to accommodate his massive size, but it is a burn I welcome because I know the bliss that is yet to come.

"Tight," he grunts, his face twisted into a pained expression that tells me he wants nothing more than to let go and fuck the brain straight out of my head, but he holds still, waiting for my muscles to relax. He is such a patient male.

The burn starts to fade, and an electric need takes its place. Waldric pulls back, almost all the way out, before sliding back in. "More," I demand, and he gives it. His hands wrap around my ankles, raising them and placing a tender kiss on one before slamming back into me.

He sets a rhythm and I match his pace, the sound of our skin slapping together filling the air. "Good?" he asks, the sound strangled.

"Mmm," I grit before moaning at the way his curved cock hits my inner walls. He growls immediately after I clench around him, his steady rock turning slightly erratic as he picks up the pace.

Lahkzo pops into my head, and briefly, I wonder if all of our sexual encounters were emotionless and cold. It certainly seems like it, and I pity Old Nalba for choosing that when she easily could have had this instead.

Then my mind drifts to Varrek. I do not want to be comparing

Waldric to past pleasure mates when his cock is filling me so deliciously, but I cannot help it. Perhaps because this encounter is beyond anything I have ever experienced. Of course, I cannot speak for the entirety of Old Nalba's time here. Maybe she had other mates besides Lahkzo that were much more enjoyable. It is hard to envision anything like this, though.

I feel Waldric's adoration for me—how much he desires my body with each thrust. With each kiss, I feel the depth of his devotion. With each growl, I feel how well he would care for me in the days ahead. I am addicted to this male. He has ruined me for other cocks.

Suddenly, he leans down and wraps his arms behind my back, lifting me and twisting our bodies until he is seated at the top of my bed, his back against the wall, and I am straddling him. His cock is still vibrating inside me, so it takes no time to pick up where we left off.

His fingers trace the raised skin of the scars on my back—scars courtesy of Yignnuf's unpredictable temper—and I avoid his questioning gaze the moment it lands on me. Instead, I reach behind me and massage his sac. Immediately, his eyes roll back in his head and his grip slides down to my ass, where his claws dig in until I feel the skin break.

Two more thrusts and we come together, his hot seed spurting into my channel in an endless stream. We flop onto our sides, our bodies sated and still connected, as we catch our breath.

"You are quite good at that," I tell him, tracing a line down his chest with my finger.

"You sound surprised," he replies, stroking my back.

"I suppose I should admit that I did not think you were . . . sexually proficient at first." He looks aghast, so I quickly add, "I am pleased I am wrong about this."

"Ah, you assumed because of my prolonged affection for you that I did not seek out any other females?" He chuckles, the sound amused and almost cocky. "I am not abstinent, pretty one." He pokes the tip of my nose, then leans in and licks it.

I join him in his chuckles, realizing truly what a foolish thought that was.

He releases his hold on me, and I whimper when he leaves my body. I watch the flex of his rounded bottom as he strides into the washroom and comes back with a clean towel. He wipes his seed from where it leaks onto my thighs, tosses the towel, and climbs back in bed. Encircling me with his bulky arms, he whispers, "Sleep deep, Nalba," into my temple before pressing a kiss to my skin.

Within moments, my body obeys.

CHAPTER 21

NALBA

The next morning, I wake with a start, frantically looking for something in my room. What that is, I do not know. I climb out of bed and rush over to the window. Throwing back the window covering, I hear Waldric groan crankily as I take in the late morning sun poking through the trees. "How long have we been asleep?" I ask without turning. We fell asleep before final meal and did not wake once.

"Not long enough," Waldric insists as he stuffs his head beneath his pillow.

He might wish to continue his slumber, but I do not. I feel . . . invigorated this day—eager to continue working on the sticky bomb until the design is perfected. Eager to protect Ekoya and strengthen her reign. Eager to eat Waldric's delicious food, and to hear more of Clohee's odd tales about Earth. Perhaps Waldric's glorious member is precisely what my body has needed since the injury. I would not be surprised to learn it has magical healing powers.

I refuse to let the dark haze of Lahkzo's words hinder my work or my mood. If there were a way to wipe him entirely from my memory without sustaining another head wound, I would do it.

Shuffling around the bed, I pull on leggings and a new tunic. I need my mane string, however, and I cannot find it. "In my pocket," Waldric mutters as he points to his pants on the floor. Reaching into his pocket . . . "Not that one. The other one," he clarifies. Reaching into his other pocket, I find three mane strings, exactly like the ones I use.

"You use these too?" I ask, surprised. I know his unruly mane is always tied into a tight knot, but I thought he used a kind of wire to hold it in place.

"No," he replies simply. When I continue to stare at him, he adds, "I keep them for you. In case you need them."

For me?

"How long have you done this?" I ask, my throat tightening with emotion.

His cheeks darken, and he pulls the pillow up slightly, so it hides part of his face. "Since the time your mane string broke while you were in line at the food hall, and your mane fell into your stew. I could do nothing to help you. I hated that feeling. From then on, I was prepared."

I wish I could remember it the way he does. I wish I could remember any of it at all.

"When did this happen?"

"Two years ago," he says quietly.

My hands drop to my sides, not knowing what to say.

"It is a silly thing, I reali–" he starts, but I leap onto the bed and kiss him hard before he can continue to downplay his thoughtfulness.

He pulls back, breathless, and laughs, pressing his forehead against mine.

"It is the least silly thing in the world," I tell him.

He kisses me again, this time plucking at my lips with his, slowly, sensually.

Then we are interrupted, once again, by the voice of a human female down in my shop. I race down the steps, throwing my mane into a high twist as I go, and find a short female with a mane the color of fire and brown spots covering her cheeks and nose. Beside her stands a tall, muscular male with shimmering blue scales, wearing a tight black shirt that matches his horns.

"Ah, Kay-teh. Nee-roh," Waldric greets from behind me. I am grateful for his presence because I had certainly forgotten their names. The fact that Nee-roh is a draxilio, however, I remembered.

"You are the draxilio," I state, uncomfortably shifting my weight between my feet. I have never been in the presence of a fire-breathing draxilio before. Well, he was on the screen pad in Kaiva's med room, but that is not the same as having him stand beneath my roof. I am not thrilled to have him in my shop surrounded by a million things that could easily be destroyed if he were to let out an ill-timed sneeze. "What is it that you want from us?"

"Relax, Nalba," Kay-teh says with her hands raised. "He's cool. I know you don't remember, but you've met my mate several times. He's not going to shift and blow your little house down. I swear."

"Little?" I repeat, taken aback by her choice of words.

"I'm sorry to bother you guys," she says, her mouth forming a sly grin. "Didn't mean to interrupt . . . anything. But, uh, I wanted to let you know that Jo sends her love, and she still feels like a total shit-burger for accidentally causing your injury."

Jo. I search my mind for the name. I find nothing. "Who is Jo?"

"Jobaki. She is a Hexrin," Waldric whispers. "You tried to assist her in the battle against Bzzsil Chi when she tried to cast a spell and Tibik interfered."

Tibik—the male I spotted on the path that gave me a bad feeling. I remember him well.

"That fucker," Kay-teh says with a bitter tone. She does not like him either? Interesting. She seems to notice my puzzled expression. "Has no one told you this whole story yet?"

"I have heard versions of it, but I would like to hear yours as well," I tell her.

"Okay, so Tibik was the lead Hexrin here, but not really. Jo let him pretend to be in charge so she could run things in peace behind the scenes. Anyway, Jo and I have been spending more time together lately. She's helping me hone my powers. I'm a witch, by the way, yada, yada, yada." She tells the story so quickly that it is a wonder she is able to breathe. "I noticed her starting to come out of her shell.

During the battle, she tried to cast a spell that wasn't part of Bruvix's plan. She knew she could do it and take the rest of Bzzsil's guards out, but Tibik tried to stop her. You saw him put his hands on her and you tackled him."

Wait. What? "I tackled a Hexrin? To protect another Hexrin?" That does not sound like me. I still do not know how I feel about Cruvo, Ekoya's mate, and he saved her life.

"Yeah! I didn't see it, but Jo has told me the story at least a hundred times. She's so grateful you intervened." Then Kay-teh's expression grows tight. "Unfortunately, while you were restraining Tibik, you got caught in the crossfire of her magic. She was trying to hit Bzzsil and the guards with her orb, but Tibik grabbed her at the last second, and the orb hit you instead. You went flying against a tree and smacked your head on a rock when you landed."

I nod as I lift a hand to feel along the edges of the wound on my head. "Right."

"Jo still feels terrible for the pain you suffered, and your memory loss," Kay-teh says, pulling something from the pocket of her long, flowing blue dress. "She wanted you to have this." She presents me with a thin black band with a golden clasp on the back. In the center of the band is a bronze wire fashioned into a hexagon shape. Inside the hexagon are four gemstones in various shades of purple, separated by an x in the center. "To protect you."

"This is supposed to protect me?" I say, my tone thick with skepticism, as she places it in my palm. It is a beautiful necklace, I must say. But I do not believe in magic. I believe in science. If there is no proof that this necklace can keep the wearer out of harm's way, then it is nothing more than a piece of jewelry.

"Oh yeah," Kay-teh says, nodding emphatically. "Jo worked really hard on making it herself, then finding the right spell to use."

"Shall I?" Waldric offers, taking the necklace from me.

It would be rude to say no. I smile in response as he steps behind me and secures the band around my neck. It is just the right size to rest comfortably around my throat without feeling too tight.

"Beautiful," Waldric whispers as he stands next to Kay-teh, admiring my new gift. "You look beautiful, Nalba."

Compliments referring to my beauty are not common. I have always been complimented on my mind, my skills, my creativity—no one was ever hesitant to shower me with kind words in that regard. But my beauty? No.

It has never bothered me that much. Beauty fades. Brilliance remains . . . unless you lose your memories, of course.

I have also never found myself to be unattractive. When I see my reflection, I am not overly pleased by what I see, but I am not disgusted by it either. I do not see flaws. Nor do I see features that are particularly striking. I see the face I was given, the body that has been formed by genetics, and the life I have lived. I just see me.

But when Waldric calls me "pretty one" or tells me I am beautiful, I cannot ignore the flutter in my stomach, or the sweat coating my palms. I am even tempted to preen under his gaze.

Running my fingers over the gemstones, I smile. Waldric seems to like it. I suppose I shall keep it for now.

* * *

"We are done," I say with the most confidence I have felt since waking in the med room. "We are, indeed, done."

"For real?" Cloh-ee asks, peering over my shoulder to look at my work.

Cloh-ee arrived this morning not long after Kay-teh and her drax-ilio mate left, and ever since, we have been hard at work on perfecting the sticky bomb's design. I have not tried to fire it yet. The testing stage happens at the very end of the design stage, especially if it is a weapon. You must be certain that it is safe to use. Or as certain as you can be without actually practicing with it.

Because of the endless hours I spent working alongside Yignnuf on weapons for Varrek's crew on Trovilia, I have a wealth of knowledge on how to safely create bombs, pistols, and swords with innovative features attached. And this might be my best work yet.

"Send a comm to Varrek and Ahlvo to let them know it is ready for field-testing," I tell Cloh-ee. I cannot wait to show Ekoya the finished product.

"Woo-hoo!" she cheers, reaching for her screen pad.

"First meal is almost ready," Waldric says as he takes a break from slicing the tree fruit and filling a bowl with berries.

"Would you like to come see my masterpiece in action?" I ask, sauntering over to his side and pressing a kiss to his neck.

"You want me to be there?" he replies, surprised by my request.

"Of course, I do."

Cloh-ee hops off her stool and wraps her cloak around her shoulders. "Varrek said they just finished with a training session, so we can head over there now."

I carefully grab the sticky bomb as Waldric and I follow her out the door.

Varrek and Ahlvo are the only warriors remaining on the training grounds. They are standing in the center, a short distance from a wooden slab propped up on a flat boulder.

Cloh-ee runs into Varrek's arms as if they have not seen each other in eons, and he lifts her into the air, spinning her around in a way that does not annoy me. I find it quite charming to see the two of them laughing and clearly so very in love.

Varrek's gaze lands on me and he gives me a friendly nod. "Nalba, I am eager to see this new device in action."

Not only will this be a weapon that Ekoya's crew can use, but we can use it here as well. Hopefully, there is no battle in our immediate future, but it is always best to prepare for the worst.

I tell everyone to take several steps back, giving me enough space to release the sticky bomb and blow up the target. Varrek stands in front of Cloh-ee on the left side, and Waldric and Ahlvo are a bit closer to me, but still behind on the right.

Taking a deep breath in, I touch the gemstones inside the hexagonal pendant lightly pressed against my throat. I do not know why I do it, but the action settles my insides and reminds me that Old Nalba may still be locked in the dark recesses of my mind, but I am still a brilliant creator with or without my memories.

I bring my arm back, preparing to release, but my thumb brushes against the outer edge, which causes a clicking sound from inside the bomb that I cannot place. Why is it clicking at all? There is no reason for it to make that sound.

"Nalba, what is wrong?" Varrek calls out, his voice wary.

I hear footsteps behind me as Ahlvo yells, "Throw it!" But his warning is too late because the sticky bomb detonates in my open palm.

CHAPTER 22

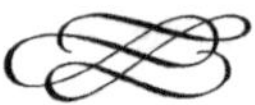

NALBA

In the med room, Kaiva goes through her aftercare instructions to Waldric and Ahlvo and I nod as if I am listening, but in reality, my mind is elsewhere. It is back at the training grounds, where everything went wrong.

The sticky bomb was ready for testing. I was sure of it. It was when the strange clicking began that I knew I was wrong. The bomb detonated shortly after that with the majority of the sharp inner material veering right, on a direct path toward Ahlvo and Waldric. Waldric's arm and neck were badly burned, and now he sits covered in bandages. Ahlvo was the luckier of the two, with minor burns on his hands.

I was the luckiest of all, however, with no wounds or burns on my body, despite being the one holding the bomb when it exploded. I have yet to determine how that is possible, but as I absently play with the hexagon pendant at my neck, I begin to wonder if I have been wrong about the Hexrins. Could this magic of theirs be real? Could their powers prove more useful than anything I could create in my shop? If so, what is the point of me? Why do I need to create anything at all if the Hexrins can mumble a few words with their hands raised and will it into existence?

These thoughts continue to rattle around my skull as Aye-vah sidles up to me. "You okay, hun?"

"I am not, Aye-vah," I reply flatly. "Not at all."

She nods, her expression sympathetic.

Dipping my chin in shame, I whisper, "I am sorry for Ahlvo's injuries. It is entirely my fault he is in pain."

"Eh." She shrugs. "The burns aren't that bad. Really. Plus, you guys heal so quickly, I'm sure they'll be gone within a couple days." She shoots me a sideways glance. "I'm more shocked that you don't have even a scratch on you. It's like Jo's your guardian angel, and she doesn't even need to be here to protect you."

"You think it was the necklace?" I ask her, astonished that a healer—a female who relies on science to do her work—so easily believes in this kind of buffoonery. "How do you explain the mechanics of that?"

"Oh, I have no explanation," she says, chuckling. "I've seen a lot of things here that defy explanation. I gave up trying to figure it out."

"But does it not bother you that your professional pursuits rely exclusively on things that can be explained and proven, and the Hexrins do whatever they wish without abiding by the same rules?"

Her gaze holds mine for a long moment, then the side of her mouth curls up in a warm smile. "I guess it would bother me if there wasn't enough room for us and the Hexrins to coexist," she says, her gaze dropping to my necklace, "but there is."

Hmm. I suppose it is only now occurring to me that I have seen the Hexrins as competition. I am not sure why, though. The coven has existed for centuries on Trovilia, and now on Oluura. There has always been a need for them, and that need has never interfered with what the inventors and healers before me have been able to offer.

"Perhaps you are right, Aye-vah," I tell her. "Thank you."

Her smile widens, then her gaze lands on Ahlvo seated on the outer med bed, looking down at his bandaged hands. "I wanna show you something." She takes my hand and pulls me over to Ahlvo, grabbing his cane and holding it out to me. "I know we told you about this already, but I thought it would help you to see it."

Ahlvo watches me with a proud gleam in his eye as I run my fingers along the intricate designs etched into the base of the cane. "Press the button," he commands. When I do, I gasp at the rapid transformation from cane to gilded sword. "See that?" he points to a design near the handle. "That is the Oluuran crest. You made it."

"An Oluuran crest?" I repeat, surprised. It is quite lovely, I must admit, with clean lines and a simple swirling design on the outside, and a grouping of trees in the center to represent our village.

"You helped bring me back," Ahlvo says, his voice quiet and heavy with emotion. "I was stuck inside my mind with dark feelings suffocating me."

"This cane reminded him of who he used to be, and who he could be again," Aye-vah adds. "I'm eternally grateful for that."

"I thank you for your kindness," I say with a sigh. "It means a great deal to me, particularly following such a monumental failure, but I—"

"Nalba, enough." Aye-vah interrupts, her expression fierce. "We believe in you. Not all of your creations are winners, but when they are, you change lives. This is just a minor setback."

I look at Waldric covered in bandages. He sees me staring and turns so he can shoot me a wide grin. In doing so, the bandages must pull at the tender skin on his neck. He winces and turns back around.

Aye-vah is correct; I do have the ability to change lives with my creations. I certainly did today. Sadly, the life I changed is the one that matters most to me, and I have caused him an incredible amount of pain.

There is no excuse for what I have done. Or rather, what I have not done. Because there must be something in my design I did not check. Something I failed to see when assembling the sticky bomb.

What frightens me is how sure I was that the bomb was ready to be tested. That there was nothing more for me to do before detonating it near a group of people I care deeply about.

Arrogance.

You will never be as good as you think you are. Remember that, Nalba. Your confidence will be your downfall.

How many times had Yignnuf said those words to me? Every time

I completed a successful project, so . . . often. He never let me celebrate a victory. He would offer a pat on the shoulder in praise, and then remind me just how inadequate I still was.

Suddenly, the memory hits. Not one I have been missing from the last five years, but from long, long ago. One I certainly wish I could forget.

I brace my shaking hands on the ground, just above my knees. Sweat pours down my back.

No, not sweat. Blood.

"How many times must I tell you this?" Yignnuf shouts, the muffled flex of the whip in his hands causing my body to jerk. "You must prioritize your creations above all else!"

I suck in a breath, knowing what is to come. I do not hear Yignnuf pull back, but the pain that shoots up my spine and out my fingertips upon his release tells me I have two more lashes to endure before I can crawl away.

"If you had spent more time reviewing the research that I have put into this type of weapon over the last two decades, instead of fraternizing with the prince, you would not have disagreed with my findings," he bellows, his breath becoming ragged from exertion.

I force myself to swallow the laughter that threatens to escape. Is this an inconvenience for him? Or too much exercise, perhaps? Abusing me with his chosen punishment tool?

But no. I must remain silent. Even a scream will earn me another lashing. I have learned that the hard way too many times.

"I-I am sorry, sir," I mumble through tears. As quickly as they fall, I wipe them away. Yignnuf is often disgusted by the display of emotions. I must not let him see my pain.

"You are sorry!" He grunts before the next one snaps at my back, tearing my skin open in long, curved lines. "Sorry? Are you truly, Nalba?"

"Y-yes, sssssir."

One more. I know there is one more. Please just do it, I want to say. Get it over with.

The thud of his boots has me pinching my eyes shut in anticipation.

I follow the sound as he circles me and stops just above where my hands still shake.

"Up," he commands.

At first, I ignore it. I know I am owed one more lashing. Surely, he has not forgotten, has he?

"Get up!" he shouts.

I scramble to my feet, careful to remain hunched over, as straightening my spine will only cause intense pain from the fresh wounds.

He tosses the whip into the corner of the dark, windowless room. Yignnuf prefers to dole out punishment on the bottom level of his facility, far from where anyone could overhear it. "I am proud you see it my way," he finally says, opening the door and gesturing for me to follow.

And the memory fades. The saddest part is the gratitude I can still feel the moment he opened that door. He gave me fewer lashings than he planned. I wanted to hug him for it. I wanted to thank him for being so gracious.

It did not matter how much he hurt me, or how often he criticized my work. I still wanted to please him. With each new project, I was sure that *this time*, he would truly be proud of me. He never was. But maybe seeking his approval was a foolish pursuit. Maybe . . . he was right all along.

Your confidence will be your downfall.

I was extremely confident in my design of the sticky bomb. Complete failure was the opposite outcome I expected today. Had I been a little less confident, had I taken the rest of the day to examine each individual component, perhaps Waldric and Ahlvo would be without burns on their skin. They would be doing the things they usually do. The things that bring them joy.

Now, here they sit, in the med room, covered in bandages.

I know they will heal. This will not leave scars on their bodies. But how will it affect their minds? Those are scars we cannot see, and my carelessness may have left them with deep ones that will never fade.

"I must go," I call out, abruptly, gaining the attention of everyone in the room. "I need to, uh, review my design. See where I went wrong."

"I'll go with you," Cloh-ee offers.

"Give me a moment. I shall come too," Waldric says, trying to roll off the bed without moving his arm.

"No, no." I wave their offers away. "This is something I must do alone." There are more protests from both of them, but I do not stay to argue. I push through the door and run back to my shop as fast as my legs will take me.

Frantically, I pull all the extra parts to the center of the table, next to the design sketch on my screen pad, and begin examining each one closely. Eventually, I notice my throat feels dry and scratchy, and too lazy to walk across the room to the spigot, I reach below the table behind me and grab the closest mug of ale.

Just one, I tell myself. I just need something to ease my throat. The first sip goes down with the signature burn of ale but is quickly followed by a warmth in my belly that causes the tension in my jaw to fade.

I scribble notes on the design, rearrange pieces, remove different components, but none of these tweaks improve the design, nor do they explain what went wrong with the first.

Old Nalba would not have been so careless.

The voice in my head is my own. I want to tell her to go away, but is she wrong? I find no evidence to counter her point.

Old Nalba healed.

Ahlvo's cane/sword is proof of that.

New Nalba only hurts.

And the bandages that now cover half of Waldric's glorious body are proof of that.

Old Nalba liked to drink ale. Lots of ale.

Ah, this is also true. Why else would she keep so many full jugs of it in her shop? As I empty one jug, I reach for another. The skies fade from the bright purples and pinks of the morning to darker shades of each, indicating it is now past middle meal.

My mind grows fuzzy with the many possible tweaks I could make to the sticky bomb. I start to repeat the different combinations, indicating I am out of fresh ideas. Sighing, I drop my head into my hands.

Old Nalba would not let emotional entanglements distract her from her projects.

Is that the problem, then? Did I allow my focus to be split between Waldric and the bomb? And if I had not, would the outcome have been different? Would his skin be free of burns? Would he be at the food hall, happily providing delicious sustenance for his clan?

When the next thought pops into my head, I fear it will haunt my remaining days.

Would Waldric be better off without me?

I want so badly to dispute the question. What have I done to deserve his adoration, though? Nothing. I have not earned his respect. I have done nothing to show him that I am worthy of his thoughtfulness. From the little insight the clan has provided, it sounds like Old Nalba was gruff, emotionally closed off, and did nothing but work, work, work.

Old Nalba did not hurt anyone.

There is no denying that.

The next sip of ale I take drains the second jug. I look down at the container, surprised I drank that one so quickly. Though, I do not hesitate to reach for the third.

Old Nalba would not either.

And perhaps that is the key to all this chaos.

I have judged Old Nalba harshly, wondering if she was truly happy in her messy shop. Maybe she was, or rather, as happy as Old Nalba could be. In her own way.

Perhaps, happiness to her meant a job well done. Perhaps that was enough.

What now, though? What would Old Nalba do, two jars deep in ale, trying to forget her own colossal failures?

Old Nalba would seek a distraction. Release.

Ah. Yes! I know just where to go for such things.

* * *

I wake to a large foot stomping on my shoulder. "Fah! Get off me, beast!" I shout, my eyes still closed. I do not know what kind of beast it is, or what it wants, but I will offer it the meat of my right arm if it will allow me to continue sleeping. Anything to get the incessant pounding inside my skull to cease. When I open my eyes, Lahkzo's face hovers above my own, and I hiss a breath in surprise. "What are you doing here? Get out!"

"Get out? You are in my house, Nalba."

His words make no sense. My eyes scan my surroundings, and I find he is correct. This is not my house. This is not my bedroom. It is his. While it is an answer, it provides no comfort. "What am I doing here?"

"You came here last eve," he explains, running a rough hand through his short silver hair. "You were very drunk. Then you started rambling on about burned skin and Old Nalba. It was all quite bizarre."

A terrifying thought occurs to me. "Did we, um . . ."

"No," he chuckles, rubbing the sleep from his eyes and crossing the room to pull back the window coverings. "I do not fuck unconscious females."

The sun shining through the window is far too bright for how much my head hurts. I wince as I cover my eyes.

"I did attempt to kiss you when you first arrived," he adds, causing my heart to drop into my stomach. "But when you pushed me away and called me 'Waldric' I realized you were not in your right mind. Then you fell asleep on the floor."

I decide this onslaught of information is too much for me to process in this state. I need to return to my shop and figure out what I should do next—which project to focus on. I scramble to my feet, wobbling a bit before regaining my balance. "I thank you for your hospitality, but I should go now."

Lahkzo stretches his arms over his head, exposing his lithe, muscular torso. There is beauty in his features, no doubt, he is just not meant to be mine. When he starts to follow me out of the room, I stop. "You do not need to walk with me," I insist. "I can find my way back."

"I was not going to do that," he says plainly. I hope whoever his inara ends up being does not expect romance. She will not get it from this one.

When we make it to the first level, we run into Waldric filling a mug with water from the spigot. He registers my presence, then his mouth falls open in shock when he sees Lahkzo behind me. His gaze drifts up, landing on my rumpled clothing and messy mane, then over to Lahkzo's bare chest. His orange eyes widen and fill with rage.

"You live here too?" I ask, not knowing what to say, but too panicked to remain quiet.

He shakes his head disapprovingly as he slams his mug on the ledge beneath the window, sloshing the water over the sides and onto the floor. Then he storms out.

CHAPTER 23

WALDRIC

"Wait! Waldric, please!" Nalba shouts as she follows me out the door of my home, close on my heels. "I can explain this!"

My claws dig into my palms as I stomp along the path. The pulling of the bandages against my burned skin is nothing compared to the pain slicing through my chest. I would endure a thousand bombs exploding in my face if I could avoid this feeling.

The sight of Nalba with Lahkzo, my housemate . . . a growl escapes my lips at the too-recent memory. Her hair mussed from sleep, or something else. Something I will not name even in my mind, as it will hurt too much.

Lahkzo and Nalba were pleasure mates before her injury. That is not new information. It did not bother me then and knowing he has fucked her does not bother me now, because I knew the arrangement did not involve emotions from either one.

But to see them together again, after all Nalba and I have shared . . . it guts me. Why do I continue to bother with this? With her?

"Waldric!" she cries out again, closer now.

I stop on the main path, turning on my heel so fast that she nearly collides with my chest. "Then do so."

"I, um," she starts, her voice shaky. Her gaze lands on my bandages and she winces. "I was in a dark place, after the explosion. I blamed myself for your suffering, for Ahlvo's. I still do. I started drinking the ale I have on hand." Her shoulders begin to shake, and she drops her hands to her sides in defeat. "I wanted a distraction from my own shame. I-I do not remember coming here to see Lahkzo. But I awoke on his floor. Nothing occurred. We did not mate. I swear it."

Nalba's eyes are filled with unshed tears—a rare sight for her. She is not one to physically express her emotions like this. It does provide some solace, but not enough for me to forget what she has done. "I believe you," I tell her honestly, before turning and stomping away.

"Wait! If you believe me, then why are you angry?" she asks, running around me and blocking my path.

"Why?" I shout back, finally letting my rage take the lead. "Because! Because after all this time. After everything, you still do not seek me out. I am an afterthought to you. Someone to pity, if acknowledged at all." Stepping around her, I continue on, eager to get away from the female who still fails to realize she holds my heart in her hands. Over my shoulder, I add, "You could have come to *me*, Nalba. But you did not."

"I felt guilty for what happened!" she replies. "You are the last person I wanted to burden with my emotional turmoil after what I did to you."

My feet stop moving. We now stand in the middle of the path with members of the clan shooting us questioning glances as they pass. If she wishes to do this now, however, I will not deny her that. The time has come, it seems.

"*You* did nothing to me, Nalba. I do not blame you for my burns. You did not cause this," I gesture to the burns hidden behind strips of cloth and medical tape. "Stop torturing yourself."

"How can I not?" she asks, her voice quieter now as she throws her hands up. "Waldric, I have no idea who I am supposed to be. Or what I am supposed to be doing. My life before my head injury is still a mystery. I just . . . I wish I could remember." Tears tumble down her cheeks, causing them to glisten in the sunlight.

I sigh, crossing my arms over my chest. She is weakening my resolve. "If you stopped worrying about what your life is supposed to be, you could live the way you want right now."

She shakes her head, her lips trembling as they form a frown. "I cannot. I tried and it led to this. To you getting hurt." She sniffles, angrily wiping away her tears. "I need to consider how Old Nalba would handle things. *She* was the brilliant one. *She* completed her projects successfully. *She* never hurt anyone. *She*—"

"*She* was deeply unhappy!" I interject.

Nalba jerks back, her brow furrowing. "What? What do you mean she was unhappy?"

She still does not understand. She cannot see beyond her own desperate quest to be who Yignnuf wanted her to be. It is time for her to let go of the memory of that terrible male.

"Why do you think you grew close with Cloh-ee? A human mated to Varrek of all people."

"I . . . I, um," she sputters.

"Why do you think you assisted in the birth of Cloh-ee and Varrek's child? Something you are not at all qualified or would normally be interested in doing."

Silence.

"Why do you think Old Nalba would leave the shop in such a mess?"

She opens her mouth to speak, but nothing comes.

"Why do you think you intervened when Jo tried to use her magic during the battle, but Tibik tried to sabotage her?"

She places her hands on her hips, her eyes darting around the path nervously. She has no answers to these questions.

"These tales of Old Nalba did not seem strange to you?"

She steps closer to me, lowering her voice in embarrassment. "There are many things that seemed strange to me about Old Nalba. I suppose I assumed she was changing. Time does that to people."

"She was miserable! You!" I shout, frustrated that she is still resisting the truth that is so clearly within her reach. "You were in a dark place as Ahlvo once was. You were working constantly and that did not make you happy. You were too exhausted to clean up after yourself. Cloh-ee tried to help you, but you would give her some excuse about everything being in a stage of experimentation.

"You allowed her into your life, but you still kept her from getting too close. That is why she was unable to tell you what you were working on before you were injured." I sigh, my cheeks and forehead hot from spewing years' worth of truths. "She was by your side each day, and still she had very little insight into what you were doing."

Nalba's gaze goes unfocused as she stares off in the distance.

"You think I did not know about you and Lahkzo?" I ask. Her eyes lock onto mine and then dip down to her feet. "Everyone knew. It did not bother me because I knew he did not care for you, nor you for him."

She bites into her bottom lip, staring intently at the dirt beneath her.

"And you liked Jo. I saw you interact with her. A Hexrin." I take a step closer, empathy making it impossible to maintain the distance between us. "You wanted more from your life, Nalba. You wanted something beyond the walls of your shop. You just did not know where to find it."

"How do you know any of this?" she asks, choking back a sob. "Why did you not tell me?"

"You never asked," I tell her simply. "And how do I know?" I scoff. "Because I have been infatuated with you since we were children. I pay attention to your needs. I listen when you speak. All I ever want is to put a smile on your face, to let you know you are more than the inventions milling inside your head."

She covers her face with her hands. I step closer and remove them. "I see you, Nalba. But you never even noticed me."

My gaze lifts to the sky, and I am reminded of all that I must accomplish this day. "I need to go," I tell her, releasing my grasp around her delicate wrists.

"Wait . . ." she cries when I begin to walk away. "Will I see you later?"

"I am not sure," I reply. "It may be best for us both to have space. For now."

She nods, despite the pout on her lips and the tears pouring from her eyes.

My body protests the moment I start walking away from her, but I ignore it. I must do this.

Until Nalba is willing to let go of her past and see me as a key part of her future, there is nothing left to say.

I arrive at the food hall to find Krahn and Ann-ah in a state of chaos—struggling to keep up with the long line of clan members eager to eat. They seem to be making progress running things, but unless they arrive long before each meal to prep the food, they fall behind. Elle-noor stands off to the side at her dish station, cleaning the dishes as quickly as they are dropped into her bin. Stepping between Krahn and Ann-ah, I help them get through the rush, reminding them of the incredible job they are doing. "This will all be solved soon. You have my word."

"Really appreciate your help," Ann-ah says, wiping the sweat off her brow with the back of her hand.

Krahn and I discuss the menu for the next handful of days, adjusting the measurements according to our current roster of people. Once Krahn is comfortable with the methods of preparing each dish, I thank him and grab a piece of petal paper from the stack next to the center fire pit and begin writing notes on it. Then I head off to my next destination.

"Morrivikka, Kaiva," I greet upon entering the med room. "I have come to see if these bandages are still necessary."

"Come, come, sweet child," she says, ushering me to one of the beds.

Aye-vah strides over as Kaiva takes off the last remaining bandage on my neck, and sucks in a breath at the sight of my skin. "It's healed so much already! That's amazing!"

"It is indeed," Kaiva agrees. "You do not need to keep the skin covered any longer. It will be good for the burns to be exposed to the air."

Precisely as I had hoped. "That is joyous news."

"You should be totally healed within a day. Maybe two, at most," Aye-vah adds.

"I thank you for your assistance," I call over my shoulder as I head for the door.

Bruvix and Vye-let are stepping out the front door of Varrek's home as I leave Kaiva's med room. "Ah, Waldric. You are ready to depart?" Bruvix asks.

Vye-let gasps at the sight of my skin. "Holy shit, are you okay? What happened?" But before I can answer, she's shaking her head and covering her mouth with her hand. "Oh my god, I'm so sorry. That's the opposite of how a person should react, and it's none of my business."

I stop her before she can continue her guilty babbling. "It is fine, Vye-let," I assure her. "Your concern is appreciated. My skin was burned in an explosion. I am healing, and these shall disappear soon."

She visibly relaxes and offers me a warm smile. "I'm glad."

"Where are your things?" Bruvix asks at the sight of my empty hands.

"I must admit, I am not quite ready. It will take me no time at all to pack, however." I gesture toward the break in the trees at the edge of the path. "Go to the ship. I shall meet you there shortly."

"Very well," Bruvix replies, guiding Vye-let in the right direction.

I race home and do not stop until I reach my bedroom. Pulling a few tunics and pairs of pants from my stack, I toss them in a soft, rectangular sack and swing it over my shoulder. When I get back downstairs, Lahkzo's eyes meet mine as he leans against the front door.

"I am sorry for the pain I have caused you, brother," he says, more emotion in his voice than I have ever heard. "I did not know your heart beats for Nalba. Had I known, I would not have continued mating with her."

"It is fine," I say. "I understand your arrangement with her was limited to physical release. I hold no grudge toward you."

He huffs a breath, leaning his head against the door. "That is delightful to my ears." Then his head snaps up with haste. "She is not your inara, correct?"

"No, Lahkzo. She is not." I stride toward him, lowering my voice to a growl. "If she were, and you allowed her into your room without alerting me to her drunken state, your cock would be lying on the floor," I point to the spot next to my foot, "right there, surrounded by a pool of blood—severed cleanly from your body."

"Understood," he replies, following an audible gulp. "It is what I would do as well . . . if I had an inara."

Lahkzo? With an inara? I am not convinced he is capable of that kind of intense love.

We exchange nods, a sign of peace between us, and he steps aside as I leave.

Lahkzo's apology sticks in my mind as I make one final stop. Perhaps he is more than I give him credit for. Perhaps he is not the only one I underestimate.

Hope surges in my chest at the latter. However, I do not have time for hope. I must get going. I continue to stand outside Nalba's shop, my hand hovering over the door handle as I summon the courage to enter.

No matter how much I long to see her face, to dry the tears that fell earlier and hold her in my arms, offering her my utmost devotion for the rest of my days, I cannot bring myself to open the door.

Thankfully, I planned for this.

Extracting the piece of petal paper from my pocket, I fold it in half and stick the corner deep into a crack in the wood. Then I press a glob of adhesive on the outer corner, ensuring the bitter wind will not blow it away.

The note explains where I will be, and for how long. I also tell her I am looking forward to seeing her when I return. I wanted to say more, but I know this is all I should say. At least for now.

Once it is secured, I make my way toward the ship. Toward Trovilia.

Away from Nalba.

CHAPTER 24

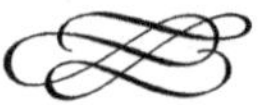

NALBA

I peek my head out the front window of my shop, admiring the deep, dark purples of the early evening sky. A violent wind whips through the air, and I tug the window closed.

Wrapping myself in a fur shawl, I walk around the tables, aimlessly, wondering for the hundredth time where Waldric is. He said he wanted space. I understand this. He deserves it after the way I have treated him.

I suppose I am surprised he has kept his word. I thought he would show up, take it all back, and insist on preparing my final meal of the day. That is the Waldric I have come to know. But it is also the Waldric I failed to notice before. That tells me it is the Waldric I do not deserve.

I am not certain I have ever felt the kind of devotion he has given me. Not from friends, not from lovers, not from family, and certainly not from Yignnuf. The love Ekoya and I share runs deep within our bones, but it is different. She has always been wild and on her own path.

It is impossible not to wonder why Waldric has remained interested in me over the years. If I barely noticed him, as he said, why did he not give up on me? What was he getting out of that unrequited love?

Unless, of course, Waldric has been lusting after a version of me he never truly knew. With the success and notoriety I gained on Trovilia with my inventions, also came many suitors. The males who tried to court me seemed entranced by this idea they had created in their minds of who I was. Most were disappointed upon getting to know the real me and discovering I am different. Some expected me to be funnier. Some assumed I was more beautiful up close. Others wanted to get access to details of top-secret projects I had not yet completed. None of them were truly interested in me.

Perhaps that is what drew Waldric to me early on, but it is clearly not what kept him interested, because it was deeper than that. He wanted to know everything I was willing to share. He wanted to get to know me so well that he could anticipate my needs. His only goal was to make me happy. He wanted to give, not take.

Tragically, the moment I learned what kind of male he is—how loving, kind, and resilient—felt like the moment I lost him.

He is probably at the food hall, assisting the others with final meal. I am not entirely interested in making conversation with the rest of the clan right now, but I will bear it if it means I can see him. Be near him.

The moment I step outside, a white object flapping in the breeze catches my attention. It is . . . paper? I am careful to dislodge it from the adhesive holding it against the door, and slowly unfold it.

It is from Waldric.

Whatever he has to say, it cannot be good. Otherwise, he would say it to my face, yes? My eyes skim through it as blood rushes to my cheeks and neck. His handwriting is disastrously sloppy—I can barely read it—but a handful of phrases jump out at me.

"Nalba...

...wish to say...I am leaving...

...with Vye-let...off to Trovilia..."

And there is one in particular that sets my blood on fire.

"...with the help of Queen Ekoya..."

A growl rips from my throat the moment I read my sister's name. She is to blame for this? My own sister has taken my ma—

Wait. No. He is not my mate. There has been no tether between us.

But that does not matter, does it? Regardless of title, Waldric is the one I wish to spend my remaining days with.

And Ekoya has taken him from me.

I turn abruptly to go inside and plan my next move, but the wind howls through the trees again and pulls the paper from my grasp. I call out in anger as I watch it float toward the sky, but I realize this is a waste of my rage. If I am to unleash my fury, I must do so with a proper plan.

The moment I see my screen pad on the table, however, all rational thought leaves my skull. I send a comm to Ekoya at once, holding the screen pad so tightly, I half expect the screen to shatter.

"Sister!" she shouts happily upon answering.

Sneering, I unleash the beast within. "You twisted, devious monster."

"Wh—"

"Do not interrupt me, traitor!" I shout. Her mouth snaps shut. "How, Ekoya? H-how could you take him from me?" My anger dissipates unexpectedly, heartbreak taking its place. "I need him, Ekoya. I n-need him."

"Nalba! You are crying?" she asks, shocked to see the tears. I never cried in front of her. I was the strong one. I had no other choice. Our mother did not want to be a mother, and our father was not around, always off on a hunting trip. "Who do you need, Nalba? What are you saying? I cannot follow."

"Waldric! Andandand . . . and you just, what? You help him leave me? You fix him up with that sour-faced human and offer a safe haven for them to flee Oluura? What else did you offer? Full use of the castle, so they may fuck in every room?"

"Nalba!" Ekoya yells back. "Shut your obnoxious face for one moment!"

That just makes me angrier.

"You cannot speak to me like this! I am a queen!" she shouts.

A bitter laugh erupts from my throat as I scream, "You are not my queen! You are the same little brat who is scared of *chunvi* birds!"

She gasps. "How dare you bring that up in this moment!"

When only the sound of my sobs fills the air, she takes a calming breath and continues, her tone steely.

"You never listen. You are stubborn. And you are the most idiotic genius to have ever existed."

"Excuse me?"

She nods. "Yes. You heard me correctly. You are an imbecile—a gigantic, unstoppable fool—if you think for one moment that I intentionally took Waldric from you, but more importantly, sister, if you willingly let him go."

My brain feels as if it is being squashed by one of Waldric's wooden spoons.

"I had no idea that you held affection for Waldric. You never spoke of him. Not once." Her voice increases in volume the more she speaks. It is a sign that her anger is growing. "Had I known, do you truly think I would try to sabotage that? Nalba, I have never seen you happy. Not about anything that does not revolve around your inventions. To be honest, I am elated to see you look like such a mess. All over a male. How delightful!"

For a moment, I think she is done speaking, but she proves me wrong. It was a silly assumption to make.

"I assume you know he is a cook? Of course, you do. He is the cook for your clan." Her tone is steadily getting louder still, but she is also talking faster. "But *why*, Nalba? Why would you not climb up that male's body and seat your cunt directly on his mouth?"

I let out a shocked cackle, not expecting such a crass statement from a queen.

"He could be serving you loaves upon loaves of steaming junasii bread wearing nothing but that welcoming smile of his, as you lie in bed." She stares at me for a long moment, then shakes her head disapprovingly. "What happened? What was it that caused you to destroy your own future with a perfect male like him?"

I do not like the image she created. Defensively, I snap, "Do you not have your own mate to bring you bread? Hmm?"

Ekoya shrugs in defeat. "You do not wish to confide in me? Fine.

What a shock that is. When you are ready to speak, you know where to find me."

The screen goes black.

She disconnected the comm.

That little monk slug disconnected the comm before I could respond. What a brat! If the pain of her death were not so fresh in my mind, I would kill her myself.

My anger dries my tears and gives me a sense of purpose. I know what to do now. And I will not fail.

Slamming the door shut behind me, I march to the food hall in search of answers. I spot Krahn, Waldric's assistant cook, but he appears to be busy serving the long line of people in front of him.

"Hey, Nalba." I turn toward the voice and find Elle-noor standing in front of me with her tiny arms crossed. "You're a real asshole, you know that?"

"Pardon, little human? What did you say?"

"Do you have any idea how much Waldric adores you?"

Ugh, this again. And from a creature half my size.

"What? Is he not good enough for you? Because he's a cook?" She jerks back, and her expression turns murderous. I would be angry if it were not so amusing. "That's some seriously fucked up, elitist nonsense right ther—"

"I know this, Elle-noor!" I shout, throwing up my hands in exasperation. "I have heard this speech already and I do not disagree! I appreciate the close bond you have built with Waldric, but I do not have time to listen to the reasons why I am a fool." Taking a deep breath, I add, "Because I must find him. Please, tell me how long ago he left."

In an instant, her grimace morphs into a smile so wide, it reaches her dark brown eyes. "Wonderful!" She pulls me for a hug I did not expect. "He left about an hour ago," she says, then pulls back. "Go get that beefy sweetheart."

"Um, yes," I reply, straightening my tunic when she finally releases me. Elle-noor possesses a surprising amount of strength. "I will."

We continue to stand there, awkwardly, without speaking. Am I waiting for her to say something? Is she waiting for me? Eventually, Elle-noor stomps her foot and yells, "Fucking go already!"

And I do. I race toward Varrek's and pound on the door repeatedly until my fist aches. He swings the door open with an irate expression. "Nalba, what is it? You know we have a baby here, do you not? What do you want?"

"Take me to Waldric. I need you to take me to him. Right now."

He rolls his eyes. Such a human thing to do. "Nalba, that is not—"

"You are not listening. I need you. To take me. To Waldric. Right now."

He holds up a hand. Is he telling me to be quiet? I will do no such thing. "He is well on his way to—"

"To Trovilia, I understand that," I explain impatiently. "I do not care. I need you to get one of our ships, launch it, and send a comm to his ship, requesting to board. I must speak with him. It is urgent, and I will not accept any answer that is not yes."

"I cannot just leave—"

"Yes! You can. Do you know how I know you can? Because you told me, Varrek. You told me that when your Cloh-ee was kidnapped by the king, that you dropped everything to travel to Trovilia and rescue her. Do you remember when you told me that?" I ask.

He nods, letting out a sigh. "I do."

"Do you also remember crediting me for talking sense into you? For convincing you to go?" Is that how he phrased it? Did he say I helped him or encouraged him? It feels so long ago now. "Yo-you said I helped you . . . um—"

"Fine! Fine," he grumbles. "I will take you. We will use the larger ship. It should catch up to his rather quickly. Just give me a moment." He slams the door shut in my face. I would be irritated if I did not hear him speaking to Cloh-ee in hushed tones. A moment later, he reappears and steps outside and I hear Cloh-ee call out, "Good luck, Nalba!" He closes the door behind him and gestures toward the break in the trees. "Let us go."

We make it to the ship in what feels like record time, but I cannot be certain of that since I have no memory of walking from the village to the area where the ships are.

Once inside, I find myself hovering over Varrek's shoulder as he pulls various levers and presses buttons, bringing the ship to life. "Nalba, you must sit," he says eventually, clearly agitated by my supervision.

Locking the safety strap into place across my chest, I absently scratch at the piece of raised metal on the seat handle. "Varrek, we need to go."

"We are," he replies, getting settled in the command chair. "You must be patient."

Patient? My mate is on another ship with a human female, the tether possibly forming between them at this very moment, and he wants me to be patient. It is an impossible request. I do my best to ignore the thought of Waldric and Vye-let together, even though it continues to enter my mind.

I just hope I reach him in time.

CHAPTER 25

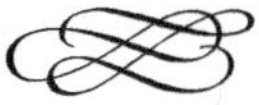

NALBA

Once we are off the ground in the ship, hurtling toward the edge of Oluura's atmosphere, Varrek clears his throat. "You and Waldric? I am glad to see this pairing."

"You are?" I ask, somewhat surprised. I have never discussed other males with Varrek. Not that I expect him to be jealous—in fact, I would be disappointed in him and protective of Cloh-ee if he were—it is just a strange topic for us. But I have no idea how long it will take to reach Waldric's ship, and it is silent in this ship to the point of being uncomfortable, so I suppose we may as well talk about it.

"Of course, I am. The entire clan has known about Waldric's feelings for you. I am happy to see something finally becoming of it."

That certainly stirs feelings inside me—namely, anger. "The entire clan knew of his feelings, and no one told me?" Then I remember that I still do not have my memories. "Or did they tell me before my injury?"

Varrek scrunches his nose, deep in thought. "I do not think anyone told you, no. Most likely because it is not our concern. How you did not realize it on your own . . . now, that is the better question."

"Fortunately, that is a question I cannot answer because I cannot remember," I tell him in a snide tone. I do not need to be called an idiot for a third time today. "Though it is certainly a mystery I wish I could solve. It makes no sense to me."

"What will you say to him?" he asks. "When you see him."

"I, uh, I do not know," I admit. I have not planned anything beyond several apologies and an offer to drop to my knees and suck his cock multiple times a day for the rest of our lives. It is not a sex act the females of Trovilia engaged in, to my knowledge, but Cloh-ee told me how to do it, and I am confident Waldric will like it. Varrek does not need to know that, though. "I shall find the words in the moment."

"I must tell you, Nalba," Varrek starts, his voice taking on a slightly shy but excited timbre, "Cloh-ee is thrilled to have a replacement vibrator on Oluura. And I am thrilled that you were able to create one for her. We have gotten much use out of it already."

I cannot help the smile that forms. "I am pleased to add joy to your mate's life in any way I can. She is good."

Varrek nods. "That she is."

After a beat of silence, Varrek perks up in his seat. "Ah," he says triumphantly. "The ship is in range. I will send a comm requesting to board." He taps several buttons, and the ship responds by beeping chaotically. I spot the smaller ship not far ahead of us. Within a few heartbeats, Varrek pulls us right up next to it. A whoosh of air sounds at the door, and it slides open.

I launch myself off the chair and through the narrow tube that connects the two ships. The door to Waldric's ship hisses open the moment I reach it, and I race onto the bridge.

There I find Bruvix manning the controls, with Waldric seated next to Vye-let.

Right.

I forgot she is here. But *why* is she here? Has Waldric already moved on? Did he want to spend this time apart with a human female on Trovilia? She is quite pretty, I suppose. Her nose is small, almost terrifyingly small, but her mane is long, and she is not much shorter than I. And she has the same curves as all the humans I have met. The males in the clan certainly seem to enjoy them.

Perhaps, it is for the best. I am sure Vye-let would not take Waldric for granted as I have. She would pro—

"Nalba," Waldric says, interrupting my disheartening thoughts, his gaze searching my face. "Why are you here?"

"I . . ." I begin. O fah! I should have prepared something to say. Ultimately, I blurt, "Why is she here?" as I point to Vye-let.

Vye-let seems to have trouble reading the situation because she smiles and cheerfully says, "Oh! I'm going back to Trovilia. Well, we both are. Do you wanna come too?"

That answers nothing.

Waldric spots my narrowed gaze and adds, "Vye-let is returning to Trovilia because she says she has found her mate. It is Queen Ekoya's head guard."

"Waldric actually looks a lot like him," Vye-let adds with an admiring grin as she looks at my mate.

Waldric gives me a puzzled look. "Did you not read the note I left on your door?"

His question reminds me of everything I wanted to say. "Why did you leave me a note? Why did you leave, Waldric? When you said you wanted space, I did not realize it meant you were *leaving*!"

He throws his hands up. "It was in the note! It was all in the note!" His eyes narrow. "You did not read it, did you?"

"Uh, do you want us to give you guys some privacy?" Vye-let asks. It is only then I realize Varrek and Bruvix are standing behind me.

"Yes," I reply as Waldric says, "Not necessary."

"I did read it," I stammer, then decide to be blunt. "Your handwriting is dreadful, and I could not read most of it, but I skimmed through it enough to . . ."

He scoffs, shaking his head disapprovingly. "Very well. Truthfully, Nalba, outside of having your meals prepared and served to you by someone else, I did not think you would notice my absence."

My jaw drops. "What?"

He shrugs.

"That is how you think I view you? As just . . . just a cook?" I ask, truly offended by what he is insinuating. I am aware I have not treated him how he deserves to be treated, but I refuse to believe it was that bad. "Some kind of lowly servant to give me my meals, and nothing more?"

"Yes," he replies, "at least in part. Because your destiny is to create." His tone is mocking as he steps toward me. "To thrive and to be known as the genius the planet needs. And my job is merely to prepare food for the masses, because . . ." he pauses, "if I were intelligent, I would do something else with my life, would I not?"

His tone is biting, and it hurts to have it used on me, but there is something about the words he used. Something that feels familiar. He has mentioned something like this before. The connection between being a cook and being smart. It is not the first time I have been confused about how they relate.

Then it dawns on me. The b'fiko syrup. When he left my shop so abruptly. But I do not recall insulting his intelligence. Did I not compliment him on being so skilled with food preparation?

He must be referring to something else. The words hover above a memory that is just outside my reach.

"You remember that, yes?"

I do, mostly, but I do not feel the guilt I probably should, had the words been mine. "I did not say that. I have never said that."

"No, you did not. Yignnuf did. He said it, and you laughed."

Yignnuf? When would he have said such a thing? And how would Waldric have heard it? We rarely ventured outside the facility. "When?"

His chin dips and he answers so quietly that I almost do not hear him. "It was many years ago. We were younger. Much younger."

"You are serious?" I shout back. It is my turn to be angry. "You have held a grudge against me *for years* because I laughed at that old prick's terrible joke? That is why you left me naked and covered in syrup that eve?"

"Wait, whaaat? I'd like to hear that story, please," Vye-let says with a chuckle.

I turn toward her. "You are still here?"

She snaps her lips shut.

I am so angry, I feel as if I could explode like a bomb inside this tiny ship. Closing the distance even more, I take a step toward Waldric until we stand a hand's width apart. "Do you know what happened when you failed to laugh at Yignnuf's jokes? Do you?"

He says nothing.

"Two lashings across the back."

His orange eyes swirl with fury. He steps forward, backing me against the wall of the ship, placing his hands on either side of my head. Then I hear metal crumple under his grasp as he grits out, "He hurt you?"

Varrek clears his throat from the doorway. "Uh, Waldric, I understand your frustration right now, but we will have to replace that panel."

Waldric does not hear him, though. His gaze is as heated as it is enraged. Perhaps I should be afraid. Instead, I feel my cunt clench around nothing, wishing Waldric was deep inside me.

Suddenly, a strange buzzing sensation forms at the base of my spine. I scratch the area, assuming it is an itch. When the feeling does not subside, my stomach twists with nerves. It spreads throughout my chest, intensifying as it goes down my arms and legs and up my throat. My vision blurs and the room starts to spin. Nothing is clear. Nothing except Waldric.

I suck in a breath.

The tether.

CHAPTER 26

WALDRIC

No. No, this blurring of my vision and electric jolt inside my chest is not what I think it is. It is not the tether. I have hoped for it to appear for so long. I will not be fooled now. It is just my anger taking shape inside my blood. That is all it is.

When Nalba inhales sharply, though, I start to wonder. When the blacks of her eyes expand, almost completely covering the gray, I wonder no longer.

"Do you feel it?" she whispers, her eyes darting between mine.

I nod, awestruck at what I am about to say. "The tether. It forms."

She chuckles, pressing her palms against my cheeks. "It forms."

I wonder why it took so long for the tether to form between us. It is not an instant thing for all mates. For some, it takes years before it forms.

Perhaps, letting go of past pain was a necessity before our souls could recognize one another. We had to clear away the anguish first, in order to begin anew as a team.

My mouth is on her in an instant. *Her. Nalba. My inara.* I can hardly believe it. If I awaken to find this all a dream, I would not be surprised. I have had many dreams like this. A possessive, primal growl builds inside my chest as I haul her into my arms and against the wall. She wraps her legs around my waist, crossing her ankles behind me.

Her claws tear at my tunic as mine fumble with the waist of her leggings. I need to feel her skin against mine. I need to plunge my cock deep inside her body.

"Vye-let, you would not know this, but what is happening between them is sacred, and physically undeniable. They will be fucking for quite some time," I hear Varrek mumble in the background. "Would you like to return to Oluura with me and depart for Trovilia a few days from now?"

"I would very much like to return to Oluura," Bruvix quickly says.

"Ugh," Vye-let groans, annoyed. "No, it's fine. I'm too impatient for that. I'll just hole up in my quarters. The ship isn't gonna crash or anything, is it? Without Bruvix at the controls? Because I have zero piloting experience."

"No, no," Varrek assures her.

My tongue is leaving a trail down Nalba's neck as I hear Varrek's footsteps cross behind me.

"I shall just check the route here . . ." he trails off. "Ah, there. If they continue to fuck throughout the remainder of your journey, you should arrive safely. Just make sure to interrupt them when it is time to land. Waldric will need to do that manually."

"How will I know it's time to land?" she asks, her voice distant, but I stop listening. My mate, my inara, is in my arms and I am never letting her go.

A whoosh from the door to the ship sounds. The electric hiss of another farther away follows it. Varrek, Bruvix, and Vye-let have left the bridge. We are alone.

I am alone with my inara.

"Wait!" Nalba gasps against my lips and jerks her head back. "I need you to know something." She swallows, and her lip wobbles as if she is about to cry. "I-I do not care about Old Nalba. How she lived or what she would want. I may not have her memories, but I do not need them. My future is by your side. I want my days to be spent within your arms. I want to eat as much of your delicious food as you will feed me." She presses her forehead against mine and sniffles. "I am honored to be your mate because you are brilliant, loving, and so very handsome. I could not ask for a more perfect male."

I kiss away the tears that fall, each press of my lips a promise that I will never make her cry.

Nalba resumes her frantic quest to strip me of my clothing. Once my chest is bare, she alternates between sucking on my skin, tracing the lines of my tattoo, and gently nibbling with her fangs.

Our bodies separate only long enough to fully undress. When my Nalba is naked before me, I see her prepare to pounce, but I step back. I sigh as I take in the sight of her. "You are the most beautiful creature I have ever seen," I tell her.

Blood rushes to her cheeks and she smiles timidly.

Elle-noor was right when she said I should compliment Nalba on other things besides her mind. It is clear she has not been told enough how radiant she is, given how stunned she always seems when I say the words. A crime, really, that she would ever question it.

Not anymore, I decide. If it takes the rest of my life to make her see how exquisite she is, my time will be well spent.

When she leaps into my arms, I do not protest. I want this as much, if not more, than she does. To solidify our bond, joining our bodies in the most sacred of ceremonies, ultimately linking our minds for eternity. I have wanted it for years.

"How do you want it?" I growl into the skin beneath her ear as I bite into it.

"Aah!" she cries out, her claws scraping against my scalp. "Floor. Let me ride you."

Her words, the promise of what is to come, send blood rushing to my cock. Pre-come pools at the tip as I guide us down, sprawling on my back. I feel the wetness of her cunt on my stomach as she writhes against me before lifting herself in order to move back. She takes my cock in hand, hissing a breath at the sight of her fingers wrapped around the head as she guides me toward her entrance.

I pull myself up to a seated position and swirl my tongue around her nipple, plucking the other with my fingers. I expect her to go slow, but my inara has never been the patient sort. I should know better. She impales herself on my cock in one smooth motion, sinking all the way down until our hips meet. "Waldric!" she roars, throwing her head back.

I thrust up into her, stars dancing at the edge of my vision as her wet heat grips me like a vise. It is the most divine sensation of my lifetime. My cock vibrates, and I feel her k'billita swell against either side of my cockhead. Her face twists into an expression of sinful agony as she attacks my neck with her lips. I do not know how long I can last. She feels too good.

Soon we are slamming into each other, my sac tightening against my body. I am close.

"Yes!" she chants, her eyes pinched closed. "Yesyesyesyes."

I will not come before her. I refuse. Luckily, I know just how to launch her over the edge. Tearing the tie from her mane, I grab as much as I can, twisting the loose strands around my fingers and fist. With my other hand, I grip the rounded globe of her bottom, delighting in the way the soft flesh fills my palm. Then I tug on her mane at the same moment that I slap the smooth skin of her ass.

She screams into the side of my neck. Her k'billita pulses against my cock as her inner walls flutter around me, gripping and releasing at a rapid pace. I come with her, my seed filling her as her cunt squeezes my cock.

Her fangs sink into the skin just above my collarbone, and my lips curl into a smile at her chosen location for a mate mark. She wants the world to know I am hers, so she marked me in a place that will be seen by all, no matter what I wear.

Where shall I mark her? My brilliant inara. Where would she want this display of commitment on her body?

Then it hits me.

I lift her wrist to my lips, pressing a kiss to her skin. If Nalba considers her mind to be her greatest asset, then her hands are second in line. They are always busy—designing, building, creating. They are always directly in her line of sight. Therefore, my mark will be visible to her at all times, reminding her that I am with her. Blood coats my tongue the moment I bite down, and I swallow it. I lick the area once I know I have gone deep enough, cleaning her wound.

We break apart, our chests heaving, our bodies slick with sweat and come. She kisses my forehead, the tenderness of it causing tears to fill my eyes. But just as quickly, the mate bond begins to work its magic, sending a heaviness and exhausted ache through my limbs.

Briefly, I consider carrying Nalba to my quarters, so she may rest on a proper bed, but the distance is too great. We roll together and land on our sides, my cock still nestled in her channel. I take her hand and bring it to my lips. "Sleep deep, inara. When we wake, our minds will be one."

"I cannot wait," she says with a smile as her eyelids flutter closed.

* * *

I wake before her. I do not know how much time has passed. All that I know is our ship has not crashed, and Nalba is officially mine. I am quite blessed.

As I gaze upon her, I cannot help but recall the many moments I wanted this to happen but was sure it never would. The embarrassing attempts at trying to woo her. The compliments I showered her with that made no sense. Could I have won her heart many years ago by merely telling her she is beautiful and offering to cook for her? I suppose it does not matter. I have her now. I will have her always.

Her eyes blink open and I feel her mind as it comes alive with awareness.

Hello, inara, I send.

She smiles sleepily, but then her eyes widen with distress. For a frightening moment, I do not know what is happening, or how to help her. But then I feel it. Her emotions dip and peak as she registers my memories, as she sees my love for her grow over time.

Then . . . something else occurs.

A pulling sensation.

No.

A gnawing.

Then a flood of images, so many that my head hurts. Wait, it is not my pain I feel. It is hers. Memories.

It is her memories. They are returning. Seeing mine must have triggered hers.

Nalba's face is impossible to look away from. Her features scrunch up tightly one moment, then relax in repose the next. Then a flash of elation. Then sadness. Then irritation. Eventually, her face settles into something more neutral as five years of memories continue to fill her mind.

I can do nothing but hold her hand and stroke her back. Then something truly wretched occurs to me. Old Nalba. With the memories comes her return. Old Nalba did not see me as anything more than a member of her clan. The cook.

Will her feelings for me change now that she has her memories? Will my failed attempts to win her heart over the years cloud the favorable image she has of me?

No, you sweet fool, she sends. *Old Nalba was a miserable crone.*

My mate squeezes my hand. When I look down, she shoots me a wink. Her pain, the overwhelming onslaught of imagery, the confusion—all have subsided, I realize.

It was you, she says. When she senses my confusion, she shows me a memory. Through her eyes, I watch a young Ekoya race ahead of her through the thickets and bushes that separate Oovahr City from the sea. Her black mane floats around her like a cloud as she breaks through the clearing, and trips on an errant lace from her boot. I feel Nalba's fear as Ekoya flies forward and lands with her face in the sand—it is visceral and suffocating. And it only intensifies when Ekoya rises to her feet and wraps her small hands around her throat as she struggles to cough. Varrek, baby-faced and lanky as he maneuvers his growing body, races over and clasps his hands together as he thrusts them into Ekoya's ribs.

I know what happens next but seeing it through Nalba's eyes is breathtaking.

I enter the scene, my mane tangled and wet from a day of swimming. Seeing Varrek incorrectly attempt the safety move we learned that very day makes me cringe. But a young Waldric steps in and shows him how to do it, and young Varrek listens.

The food that was lodged in Ekoya's throat flies across the sand, and I can remember how relief washed over me at that moment. I feel it even now.

It was you, she repeats.

It was me, I reply.

She tilts her head, giving me an indecipherable look. *I pity Old Nalba,* she sends. *She had everything standing right in front of her, handing her extra slices of bread.*

I laugh at the absurdity of assuming extra bread would be enough to win her over.

She nods. *It is quite silly when you think about it.*

What? I ask. *The extra bread?*

No, she sends back. *That I needed to be thrown into a tree and hit my head on a rock to truly open my eyes.*

Mmm. Quite a violent and dramatic way to change your way of thinking, I tell her. *Have you always been so stubborn?*

You know I have, she sends back with a chuckle.

I do indeed.

She pulls herself up until our lips are almost touching. Then she whispers, "Good thing you are the smart one."

EPILOGUE

NALBA

A scent fills my nose, pulling me from a deep, restful slumber. I flare my nostrils, trying to determine the source of the sweet, rich fragrance.

O fah! I was hoping to surprise you, Waldric sends. A moment later, the door to our room is thrown open. In his hands, he carries two plates piled high with what looks to be a variety of baked sweets.

Yes, you are correct, he replies. I have not entirely gotten used to having someone else in my head, but his instinctual kindness has provided a much-needed shift in tone. He is much nicer than the voice inside my head, whether it is my own or Yignnuf's. At the thought of my former mentor, I feel Waldric's anger flare. *That decrepit waste of skin. If the virus had not taken him, I would have been honored to stop his heart.*

Well, he is much nicer *most* of the time.

Did you make these? I ask, eager to change the subject. He hands me my plate, and I quickly take a bite of the biggest item on top of the pile.

No, he replies. *These were baked by our new clan members, Jahto and Denya. Well, soon-to-be clan members, I should say. I am still trying to determine their strengths before we bring them back to Oluura. I think Denya will do well with meats, and Jahto seems to be keen on stews. But they both enjoy sweets, which the humans will certainly appreciate.*

My fangs sink into a thick top layer of hardened *muuhn*, and I moan at the familiar, decadent taste.

Good, yes? he asks. When I nod enthusiastically, he adds, *The muuhn seems to match the description Ann-ah gave of a human food called fraws-ting, which she was very eager to start adding to her space muh-finns.*

Waldric and I share our thoughts on each baked treat as we lounge in bed. He tells me more about Jahto and Denya, the different cooking tests he has given them over the last two days, and how thrilled they both seem to be joining our clan.

Once our plates are clean, Waldric takes my hand and pulls me out of bed. I whine in protest, but he guides me to the large window in our room overlooking Oovahr City. I forget my disappointment altogether and sigh at the view.

I cannot believe this is all hers. Ekoya. Queen of Trovilia. It is still so strange to me, I send.

I do not disagree, he replies with a wave of fondness and amusement. *She was always such a fearless little thing. I suppose that is part of what makes her a good ruler.*

The comments from the council meeting I snuck into last eve rise to the surface, filling me with dread. *Not everyone thinks she is a good ruler. The continued assassination attempts worry me. I know her crew is made up of newly recruited warriors, and the misogynistic trouble-makers who served the king are gone, but . . .*

It will not come to that, Waldric interrupts my thoughts with the unwavering confidence he has in Cruvo, Ekoya's mate. *He will not let any harm come to her.*

"Morrivikka, sister!" Ekoya hollers as she enters the room. Cruvo follows closely behind, brushing his maroon mane—the signature color of all Hexrins—out of his eyes. It is cropped on both sides of his head, and long on top. It makes his pointy ears and many piercings that much more prominent.

Speaking of, I send to Waldric.

He sends me an image of Ekoya and Cruvo rubbing their noses against each other as if no one was looking during final meal yesterday, where we celebrated the finalization of the peace treaty between Trovilia and D'Alluk.

I was not prepared to find them so utterly adorable, but their love is impossible to discount or deny. Not that I am putting effort into either anymore. My resentment toward Cruvo from when he and Ekoya were newly mated was nothing more than misdirected jealousy. I missed my sister, and he got her all to himself.

But then we thought she died. We both grieved, separately, but eternally linked by that agonizing loss. He went on to risk his life in an attempt to save hers. He was successful in that. Now she is queen, and he is happy to stand at her side, giving her the space and support to rule a planet while he uses his powers to keep her safe from harm.

Cruvo is family, Waldric adds. *I am delighted to have a brother.*

I had never thought of Cruvo as my brother. I suppose that is another glaring truth that I could not see.

Waldric leans down and kisses my temple. *You see it now. That is all that matters.*

"I wish you did not have to depart so soon," Ekoya says as Cruvo stands behind her playing with her mane. At one point, he takes a step back, his brow furrowed, before straightening her crown. It is a subtle act, one Ekoya did not even register but caused my throat to tighten at the tenderness of it.

"As do we," Waldric replies. "But we must return today. We have had a wonderful time visiting you. You must come see us soon on Oluura."

"Ooh, we shall!" she exclaims, clapping her hands together. "I would love to see your village."

"Is Vye-let settling well here?" I ask Ekoya. We have not seen her since we left the ship upon arrival.

I am surprised you remembered her existence at all, Waldric sends.

It is hard to forget the female I previously thought was stealing my mate from me, I reply.

"Yes! She is thrilled to be back here," Ekoya says. "I had not realized the tether formed between her and Polek, but seeing them together now, there is no doubt." Then her head tilts as she stares at Waldric and me, her expression warm. "You are a glorious match," she finally says.

"Agreed," Cruvo adds with a nod.

He speaks, I send Waldric with a note of sarcasm.

He chuckles inside my head, replying, *Those who remain quiet are often the ones with emotions as deep as the sea. Do not underestimate them.*

It is a valid point. Once again, I am grateful to have this male inside my head.

Even if I distract you from your work?

Especially when you distract me from my work, I reply. *How am I supposed to make new memories if I never leave my shop?*

He sends me a mental gasp. *I will remind you of this when we get home.*

I squeeze his hand, silently thanking him for loving me. *Do not ever let me forget.*

* * *

Thank you for reading HEALING HIS MATE! I hope you loved Nalba and Waldric's story. Are you wondering how Jo has been faring at Kate and Niro's caves? What about her Happily Ever After? Good news! You're about to find out!

Start reading ENCHANTING HER MATE now!

ALSO FROM IVY

<u>ALIENS OF OLUURA</u>

Saving His Mate

Charming His Mate

Stealing His Mate

Keeping His Mate

Healing His Mate

Enchanting Her Mate

(This series isn't finished. There's plenty more to come!)

<u>STRANDED ON EARTH</u>

Her Alien Bodyguard

Her Alien Neighbor

Her Alien Librarian

Her Alien Student

Her Alien Boss

ENJOY THIS BOOK?

Did you enjoy this book? If so, please leave a review! It helps others find my work.

Get all the deets on new releases, bonus chapters, teasers, and giveaways by signing up for my <u>newsletter</u>.

FROM IVY

There's just something about Nalba, am I right? Her brutal honesty and unyielding confidence have made for some hilarious moments in books 1 through 4. But how do you make a character like that, someone who needs no one, truly likable? How do you set the stage for her to fall in love?

Well, you could do what I did, and toss her against a tree, leaving her with a massive head wound that has knocked five years of memories out of her head! In order for her to stop ignoring Waldric and open her damn eyes, I needed to put Nalba in a very vulnerable state, and I'm a total sucker for amnesia romances, so that's the path I chose. Amnesia provides a fresh start, in a way, and that's what our brilliant inventor required in order to see what was really in front of her.

I also wanted to provide some insight into why Nalba comes across as cold. Why she's so driven and emotionally closed off. It's not because she's heartless. It's actually a trauma response from her time as Yignnuf's apprentice.

As for Waldric, as much as I've always loved our sweet cook, he needed a push to let go of his insecurities and gain some confidence in the job he loves doing. Cooking for just Nalba, as opposed to the whole clan, and watching her memories return upon eating his food, reinforced how crucial his role is among the clan. It also helped combat the memory of Yignnuf mocking the role and Nalba laughing.

So what now? Who's next? If you guessed Jo, you were right! It's time for our timid, secret coven leader to embrace her power, and for a goofy, fearless draxilio to show her a kind of magic she's never felt before. Jo and Alu will get their HEA's in book 6, *Enchanting Her Mate*!

Plus, Alu isn't the only dragon to find her mate. We've got two others on Oluura who are about to find theirs. Stay tuned!

Love,

Ivy

P.S. - A special thank you to my amazing editors, Tina, Mandi, and Jenny, who turn my sometimes nonsensical words in to something beautiful.

And to you, my dear readers, for supporting my work and gobbling up my books the moment they go live. I wouldn't be here without you.

RESOURCES

SAMHSA (Substance Abuse and Mental Health Services
Administration Hotline)
1-800-662-HELP (4357)
TTY: 1-800-487-4889
samhsa.gov

National Suicide Prevention Hotline
1-800-273-8255 (call or chat)
suicideprevention.org

National Domestic Violence Hotline
1-800-799-SAFE (7233) (call or chat)
thehotline.org

ABOUT IVY

Ivy Knox has always been a voracious reader of romance novels, but quickly found her home in sci-fi romance because life on Earth can be kind of a drag. When she's not lost on faraway worlds created by her favorite authors, she's creating her own.

Ivy lives with her husband and two neurotic (but very cute) dogs in Chicago. When she's not reading or writing, she's probably watching *What We Do in the Shadows, The Good Place,* or *Fall of the House of Usher* for the millionth time.